Grounded in July

THE SEQUEL TO GROUNDED IN JANUARY

SAVANNAH HENDRICKS

GRAND BAYOU PRESS

First published by Grand Bayou Press 2021

Library of Congress Control Number: 2021909670

ISBN 978-1-7344553-4-2 *** ASIN B08RC99X4P

Cover design by Red Leaf Book Design - https://www.redleafbookdesign.com/

Editor: Mary Dunbar

Annually, 10% of the proceeds from the sale of this book, and all Savannah's books are donated to dog rescue organizations.

READING IS BETTER WITH A DOG ~ Savannah

For those with multiple sclerosis, never stop loving, and never stop being loved.

Preface

The most popular question readers ask about **Grounded in January** is why I wrote a story about multiple sclerosis. I never set out to dive into the adult fiction market with a novel centered around MS, but I welcomed the idea in 2017 when I began plotting **Grounded in January**.

My mom was diagnosed with MS in her late twenties, and growing up, watching the symptoms take over her life, was eye-opening and scary. I have no memories of her standing or walking, as she was in a wheelchair for as long as I can recall. But my mom always had a smile, and others commented on the joy she showcased.

When the idea of Ox's story came about, I had to make sure that I captured multiple sclerosis correctly. Yet, I wanted Ox to follow a different outcome than my mom dealt with.

Back in the late 1970s, when my mom started showing signs, there wasn't much known about MS. Thankfully, each year doctors and researchers are making advances.

I think about all the things my mom missed out on because she passed at the young age of forty-three, which would include the invention of DVDs and having the ability to rewatch M*A*S*H at her leisure.

My mom taught me a lot in a short time. She made sure I understood it was impolite to eat in front of others if they weren't joining you, and please and thank you bites were the rule — not an exception.

The world is not always a happy place, and memories can break our hearts. This is why Ox's story continues to have a positive outcome while still being true to the diagnosis. I only wish my mom's outcome had been different.

Contents

Chapter 1

"Bayou, give that back," Kate Swanson warned the yellow English Labrador.

Her long curls fell forward as she lunged left and then right in a sumo-squat position.

The dog's tail swatted back and forth while his paws danced in place, preparing for a mad dash.

"Ox!" Kate shouted for her husband of only a year.

Oxnard Swanson staggered across the Inn of the Woods' living room with a cane in his right hand. "What's going on?"

"Bayou has my Croc, again." Kate faced the dog with the pale blue shoe, in sport mode, clenched in his jaw like a piece of wild game he caught.

"You insist on wearing rubber toys on your feet." Ox snickered.

"They're incredibly comfortable shoes, and you know it."

Wearing only one Croc, Kate took two steps forward as Bayou went right. Then the dog backed up two paws and shuffled to the left. His eyes appeared to smile at her with delight for the game.

Kate spun around and fell onto her bottom as he jetted past, heading for the entryway. "Bayou Swanson!"

"Do you think calling him by his first and last name will make him listen better? I don't think it's the same as a child."

Ox remained between Kate and Bayou, dressed in jeans and a solid black T-shirt. "I wonder if next year's version will include a squeaker in the heel."

"It's a good thing you're handsome, or I wouldn't put up with your jokes." Kate's focus remained on Bayou, sprawled out on the entryway rug, the Croc on end between his front paws.

"I have jokes?" Ox rubbed his chin like a philosopher posing for a statue.

Without paying attention, Kate stepped up from the sunken living room. However, her right foot didn't clear the step entirely, and she stumbled in an attempt to correct her balance. She sprinted to stay upright, reached for the staircase railing, and grabbed hold.

"Are you okay?" Ox placed his hand on the small of her back.

She tucked her curls behind her ears and yanked down her hiked-up periwinkle T-shirt. "I might need your neurologist to write me a script for a cane as well."

Her husband laughed, and she went to her tiptoes and kissed his lips. She never tired of showing him how much she loved him. And kissing him was her most favorite activity in the world. Although Ox would say being clumsy was her favorite activity.

"Are you sure you don't want me to drive you to your doctor's appointment?" Kate watched Bayou rest his chin on the Croc as though his goal all along was to use it as a pillow.

She reached down to steal its mate back from Bayou, but he pressed his chin into it. It was like trying to free a shoe stuck under an eighteen-wheeler's tire. "Fine, have it."

Kate made her way into the kitchen and flung open the refrigerator. She removed a pitcher of iced tea with slices of lemon floating on the top.

"You know how much I hate going; I don't need you dealing with it too." Ox ran a hand through his hair. "Stay here, enjoy the quietness. Matt and Ali will be arriving tomorrow, and we'll be busier than bees on a new blossom."

"I'll be busier than a bee. But, your buzzy-self will be resting."

She didn't need to remind Ox of the importance of relaxing; he already knew, but she struggled to shake the habit.

His multiple sclerosis symptoms had been rough on him the last few months. And while Kate did her best to help out, it frustrated Ox. He'd been napping more, dropping more things, and he'd even taken a nasty fall the other morning.

"I'll be fine." Ox checked his wristwatch. "I better get going, though."

"Make sure you let me know when you're heading home so I can start dinner. I'm making my less-dairy chicken lasagna tonight." She removed a glass from the cupboard, poured herself some iced tea, and returned the pitcher to the refrigerator.

"My new favorite dish." Ox moved his hand to his front pocket, most likely checking for his cell phone. "I think I have everything." Then he touched his back pocket, where he kept his wallet.

Kate had spent a lot of time researching the effects of food on the symptoms of MS. And after reading about how dairy could affect those symptoms, she'd been modifying recipes.

Ox loved lasagna. However, most recipes were at least fifty percent dairy-heavy, and she'd been experimenting with keeping the taste while removing as much cheese as she could.

Ox gathered up his keys and patted his leg for Bayou to come to him.

"My two reasons to get back home as quickly as possible." He winked at her and petted Bayou, now standing next to him.

You could have three reasons.

She carried her glass with her and opened the front door. "Are you sure you don't want him to go with you?"

"I need to pick up my prescriptions on the way back, and if the drive-thru is still closed, I can't leave him in the hot truck."

She kissed his cheek. "Drive safe. I love you."

He stepped outside and looked at Bayou. "I love you." Then his eyes moved up to his wife. "I love you too, Kate."

She crossed her arms and fluttered her eyelashes.

"What?" Heading down the three long front porch steps, he gripped the railing with his left hand and the cane in the other hand. "I'm just going in order of shortest to tallest for I love you's."

He paused at the bottom and turned around, grinning. "Now, don't hurt yourself while I'm gone. I know it's a challenge."

Kate groaned and gave a wave before she closed the door. She leaned her back against it and took a deep breath. Bayou pushed his face against Kate's knees and wedged his back end between her legs.

She stroked his soft buttery yellow fur. "I hate him driving himself all the way there and back, but you know how stubborn he can be."

She gazed down, and Bayou looked up at her, the top of his head pressed against her thighs. "I love you too."

With that, Bayou wandered off into the living room, and Kate noticed the Croc was no longer on the entry rug. She searched under the credenza and around the coat rack, hoping to find where he'd hidden it.

"Maybe if you had a sibling to play with, you could leave my shoes alone." Kate wiggled her toes in the one she had on. "They might be ugly, but they're so comfortable."

Heading into the living room, she couldn't help but stare at the view out the windows. A sense of peace washed over her. It didn't matter how many times a day she stopped to admire the scenery; it was the same delightful feeling.

Washington's spring had transformed into summer, and the trees showcased their greenest of greens. The valley below was littered with cedar, fir, and cypress trees. Their branches intertwined, causing their leaves to appear like an ocean of emeralds.

Kate rested her hand on the massive wood-framed window and sipped her iced tea. A slice of lemon tickled her upper lip. The sun wouldn't set until just after nine, and Kate loved this about the summers here.

Tonight, as long as Ox felt up to it, they could snuggle up and watch the sunset on the back deck. Having a break from the guests and spending time alone was rare, especially during the peak summer season. With her photography business continuing to grow, time alone proved harder to come by. And with Ox's diagnosis taking its toll on him, they decided they'd shut down the inn for a week. That was when Kate had the matchmaking idea to invite Ali and Matt for a visit.

She missed her best friend, and although her fear of flying had improved by at least eighty percent, the thought of flying over the ocean still paralyzed her with worry. However, by inviting Ali, along with her non-existent dating life, Kate could avoid flying. And with Matt still single, sparks began to dance in her mind about what a great match they might make. Therefore, even though she and Ox needed downtime, she couldn't help but jump on an opportunity to create a love connection.

An unexpected knock at the door caused Bayou to bellow a single bark. Startled, Kate sloshed the glass of tea in her hand. She wiped off the spill running down the outside with the back of her hand as she hurried to the front door and eased it open.

"Maggie." Kate smiled.

The once regular out-of-town guest was now a full-time Crooked River resident. Ox and Kate spent at least one dinner a month with Maggie and Ox's long-time family friend, Richard.

Maggie gave a quick hug, and Kate motioned for her to come inside. Her gray hair grazed her shoulders, and her rose lipstick added a pop of color.

After the sudden passing of Richard's wife, he and Maggie got to know each other at her and Ox's wedding. And a few months ago, Maggie had moved to Washington after her long-distance relationship with Richard blossomed like a flower yearning for sunlight. Anyone would be hard-pressed not to notice their second chance love growing.

It wasn't like her to come over unannounced, and Kate worried something might be wrong.

"I'm sorry to drop in like this, but I wanted to ask you and Ox something important." Maggie squeezed her hands together as though they were cold. "Why are you only wearing one shoe?"

Kate glanced down at her Croc. "You'll have to ask Bayou."

The dog made it known he needed some attention before Maggie could move past the entry rug.

She bent over and gave him a quick head pat. "Hi, Bayou."

"Ox is at a doctor's appointment right now." Kate placed her hand on Maggie's arm. "Is everything alright? Is Richard okay?"

Maggie waved her hand in the air. "Goodness, sorry to worry you. Yes, we're good. But, gosh, I don't think I can wait another minute." She wiggled her hand in front of Kate's face.

"Oh my goodness." Kate grabbed Maggie's hand and pulled it close to her face. "Is that—"

Maggie blushed. "Richard asked me to marry him."

Wrapped around her finger was a simple gold band. But, as Maggie's hand shifted with joy, you'd have thought it was adorned with a million diamonds.

"I know it's only a gold band, but love trumps diamonds."

"It's perfect." She let go of Maggie's hand. "Were you surprised?"

Kate motioned for her to come into the kitchen and pulled out a barstool at the island.

Sitting down, Maggie held her hand out, continuing to admire it. "I was. It was completely unexpected."

Kate stood at the refrigerator. "Can I get you something to drink? I have iced Earl Grey, your favorite."

"Thank you. I'd love some." Maggie rested her elbows on the island's black granite with peacock green veins running through it.

Kate poured the tea into a wide-mouth mason jar and set it in front of Maggie. Then, before putting it back, she topped off her glass.

Bayou flopped on the floor at the end of the island; that way, if Kate or Maggie got up, he wouldn't miss a thing.

Kate glanced at her wedding ring, an oval diamond with an interwoven pave band design, thinking back when Ox proposed.

It'd been a beautiful evening, sitting on his tailgate like two teenagers while Bayou snored on the blanket behind them. The night's sky was lit only by the half-moon, and the low glow from the stereo's display inside the truck allowed for a beautiful view of the stars.

"I might as well come right out with it," Maggie announced as she looked up from her ring. "Richard and I don't want to wait."

"Wait?" Kate blinked, holding her eyes closed a few seconds longer than usual.

"We want to get married this month."

Kate's mouth formed an O. "Are you two going to Las Vegas to elope?"

Maggie laughed and shook her head no. "I should wait for Ox to return so that I can ask you both, but I guess even age doesn't change your excitement." Maggie smiled as her eyes lit up. "Richard and I want to get married here, at the inn."

Kate set down her glass and pressed her hands on the island. "Here?"

Maggie laughed. "Yes, this inn is perfect. I know Richard and I didn't meet here, and while this was Stan and I's vacation spot, it's a connection with the past and the present. The inn has caused us all to unite, in one way or another. Richard and I discussed it, and we agreed this was the best place for our wedding. If it weren't for the Inn of the Woods, I never would've met Ox's parents. I never would've met you. Or watched you and Ox fall in love, and because of those things, I was led to Richard. This place should be renamed the Inn of Love."

Maggie turned around in her chair. "And it's just big enough to host a small reception if you can even call it that. We want to get married on the sixth. Seven-six-twenty-twenty-one. Seven and six equals thirteen; it's our lucky number. Do you think Ox will be up for it? Will you host us?"

Kate bit at her fingernail. "Matt and Ali, you remember them, they're arriving tomorrow. And we have all the rooms booked for right after they leave."

She hated being rude and didn't want to tell Maggie that Ox had a flare-up with his MS. Preparing for a wedding might be too much to take on. Yet, it's not like marriages happen every year, at least she hoped not, and Maggie had done so much for Kate, helping her get her photography off the ground.

"We won't need any rooms." Maggie took a long sip of tea.

Kate forced a smile as she scolded herself for being selfish. "Great, then we'll make it work."

"Perfect," Maggie declared. "We'd love to include Matt and Ali. It'd be a great way to get to know them better. And do I sense possible matchmaking going on? Last I heard from you, they're single."

"Your memory is spot on."

"How fun." Maggie stared off and sighed. "It's going to be perfect."

Kate half-smiled before hiding her mouth behind her glass of iced tea. *What can possibly go wrong with an intimate last-minute wedding?*

Chapter 2

Ox pulled his truck into the garage and shut it off. He slumped back and pressed his head into the headrest. The lengthy drive home from the neurologist's office hadn't been long enough to calm his frustration.

He punched the ceiling of his truck. Then, keeping his fist clenched, he tried to ignore the numbness in his fingertips. Ox was unaware his nails were digging into his palm until he saw the half-moon marks upon release.

Trying some breathing exercises to lower his heart rate, he inhaled and exhaled in an attempt to forget the words that spilled from the doctor's mouth as though in slow motion. Unfortunately, the entire drive home, those words played out like a nightmare on repeat, causing him not to recall how he even made it back to the inn.

Ox leaned on his cane as he climbed from the truck. The daytime running headlights reflected off a piece of metal in the corner. A front-wheeled walker and wheelchair, both folded up, hidden as best as possible behind a box labeled: Christmas decorations.

About four months ago, after a series of falls, his neurologist prescribed the devices. When they arrived from the insurance company, he immediately shoved them out of sight. He kept the faith that his severe leg weakness was a one-time ordeal, and he'd never need anything other than his cane to get around.

Ox made it out of the garage, cane in hand, and spotted the outline of his wife and loyal dog waiting at the open front door.

Lining the walk and running the length of the front patio were coral blush azaleas and azure blue hydrangeas. Once a week, Kate spent lazy afternoons tidying up the bushes and cutting them to fill vases for the guests' rooms. Ox had worried about keeping the plants after bringing Bayou home since they're toxic to dogs. Thankfully the Lab never so much as sniffed them.

"You missed Maggie," his wife mentioned as he climbed the steps.

Bayou's tail wagged, and he greeted Ox with a sniff—attack on his shoes and then his pants.

"What did she stop by for?" He leaned down and kissed Kate. Her lips were soft and tasted of lemon.

"Maybe you should sit down first." She placed a hand on his back as they made their way inside and headed for the kitchen.

He pulled out a chair at the table and rested his cane against it. "That bad?"

The scent of pasta sauce, cheese, and fresh bread filled the kitchen. Kate's famous boule of crusty Dutch oven French bread rested on the cutting board. He noticed a side piece of the bread was missing. Kate was never one to wait for it to cool before she snacked on a slice.

"Not bad, but I want to know how your appointment went." She sliced off two pieces and brought them to the table.

The bread stretched in his fingers as he tore off the crust and folded it into his mouth. There was no point in delaying the news. She'd figure it out within a few days on her own. Yet, he couldn't say the words aloud. The simple thought of them tore at his chest. "You go first."

She rested her elbows on the table. "Maggie and Richard are engaged."

"That's great." Ox tore off more bread. "And I needed to sit down for that?"

Bayou sighed as he laid between him and Kate. Ox tossed the dog a piece of bread that he snatched up like Jaws.

Kate poked at the pockets of air in her slice. "They want to get married here."

"I don't see a downside to this. I think it would be great to host the wedding. We've never done one at the inn before."

"It's this week." Kate's face went slack.

"This week?" Ox's forehead wrinkled as he pushed his pointer finger into the tabletop. "As in *this* week?"

"The sixth."

The oven's timer buzzed, and Kate got up to silence it.

Bayou followed behind for moral support, or more likely morsel support, just in case she dropped breadcrumbs along the way.

Kate slipped on the oven mitts, removed a rectangular glass dish with foil draped over it, and set it on top of the stove. She pulled the foil back as steam rose from the lasagna.

"I don't understand the rush; it seems sudden." Ox ate the last piece of bread on his plate.

"She doesn't want to waste any time. I can understand. I think when you *really* know, why wait? And the math for the date totals thirteen, so they think it's a sign. Anyways, Maggie said it was fine with her if Matt and Ali were to join in."

"How many guests?"

Kate tossed the foil into the trash can under the sink. "She didn't say, but either way, none are staying here. We're simply hosting the wedding and a small reception."

"Not a lot of notice, but it's doable and not the end of the world." *Unlike my news.* "Why were you acting like it was a bad thing?"

"You've been tired lately, and with our friends coming in, I'm worried it's going to be too much for you."

"You need to stop worrying about me. I'm fine." He sighed through his nose.

She turned the oven setting to broil and slid the dish back into the top rack to crisp the thin layer of cheese.

Ox's mouth watered, and for at least a few seconds, all he thought about was how hungry he was and not the horrible news he had to tell Kate. "You told Maggie we'll do it, right?"

"Of course. You should've seen her; she was like a teenager getting ready to go to prom. But it means I'm going to be beyond busy. I also have those photos due."

Ox watched her curls cascade over her shoulders, causing him to want to forget about everything else in the world and cuddle with Kate on the couch. Simply shut off his mind and wrap his fingers around a copper curl and breathe in the scent of her ginger conditioner.

"Ox?"

He stared at her as she waved a wine glass near him.

"Did you want wine?"

"No, thanks, sorry." He regained his focus. "Look, it's not like I won't be here to assist. We'll figure it out. We always do."

Kate shrugged her shoulders, and he knew something else had to be bugging his wife. A small wedding with their friends would not cause Kate to act off. Lately, she'd been gazing off into space and seemed absentminded during movies.

Pressing her palms on the counter, she stretched forward, the freckles shown at the V of her shirt. He marveled at her beauty, even when she was flustered.

"Ox, I don't know about this wedding."

"Come here." He waved her in his direction.

She made her way over, and he took her hand as she lowered herself onto his lap. He pushed her hair behind her right ear.

Swallowing the lump in the back of his throat, he looked her in the eyes. "I'm going to have a lot of free time now. I can help you with the wedding and everything else."

"Everything else?" She rested her head on his shoulder, and he breathed in her soft, peony perfume she always dabbed across her collar bone.

For a few seconds, he didn't respond. Ox closed his eyes and listened to his wife's breathing, soon falling in rhythm with his.

Kate lifted her head off his shoulder. "What do you mean everything else?"

"The neurologist grounded me." Ox choked on the words. "He's pulled my pilot's license."

Chapter 3

She pulled her husband as close as she could and squeezed her arms around him as though doing so would make the devastating news disappear. "Babe, I'm so sorry."

Tears streamed down her cheeks as she used all her inner strength to keep from sobbing loudly. His neurologist had instantly stripped the one true joy from his life, and she'd hoped they would never see this day.

Ox shifted in his chair, and Kate knew she needed to stand up as his legs were probably hurting.

She wiped her tears, and dizziness swept over her. If the news was affecting her so strongly, Kate couldn't imagine what Ox was going through.

"Babe," she started, "why didn't you call me on the way home?"

"I didn't know what to say." Ox rubbed the top of his thighs with his palms. "I still don't." He smacked the top of his legs. "I've lost control of my life. I'm becoming everything I feared, limited and helpless."

There was no appropriate way to respond to make him feel better. Whatever she said would not fix the situation. But she couldn't stop her heart from ripping in two.

Kate popped open the oven door a smidge to check on the lasagna and wiped the remaining tears away with the oven mitt. The cheese had turned golden brown, so she removed the dish with the potholders and set it on the stovetop.

Bayou sensed Ox's emotions and turned to him. The Lab rubbed his face against Ox's knees before lying down across both his feet.

"He'll end up pulling my driver's license if I continue to decline."

"But he *hasn't* done that." Kate went to open the cupboard but turned to look back at Ox. "It's going to be okay."

Pulling open the door, she turned back to face it as the door smacked her on the cheek.

"Ouch!" she shouted.

She heard Ox's footsteps coming towards her. "Did you just punch yourself with the cupboard door?"

"No." Kate pressed her palm against her cheek. "Yes."

He muffled a chuckle and placed a hand on her shoulder. "You're not bleeding or missing a tooth, are you?"

She looked up at him and ran her tongue over her teeth. "I don't think so."

Ox kissed the top of her head and then the tip of her nose. "Let me get what we need. If the door is *that* violent, I'd hate to see what the dishes have in store for you."

He removed two plates from the cupboard and set them next to the bread on the island.

"Back before the cupboard rudely interrupted us, I wanted to say I know it's hard not to focus on the news of today." She removed a spatula from the drawer. "And I wish there was something I could say or do about you being grounded that would be a positive."

"But there isn't," he snapped. "This is precisely why I didn't want to get ma . . . "

She swallowed and pressed her lips together to keep quiet. Ox was right; discussing it wouldn't do any good because he had every right to be upset. And no matter how much they talked about it, nothing would bring his license back.

But was he about to say that's why he never wanted to get . . . married? Her hands trembled, and her breath seemed to catch in her throat.

Anyone who thought multiple sclerosis was a solo diagnosis was dead wrong. Like any other disease, it affected the patient and anyone who loved the person, leaving everyone feeling helpless. But she couldn't let go of the thought about what Ox stopped himself from saying.

"What about Bayou?" Ox pointed at the dog asleep at the base of the kitchen table. "All the training we went through. And you know how much he loves to fly. It's not like you'll be taking over for me."

While Kate knew he didn't mean to sound snippy, the words still stung. Sure, she'd come a long way with her fear of flying, yet he made it seem as though she could've saved him and Bayou's dreams if it wasn't for her anxiety.

"Let's eat dinner before it gets cold," the words choked out over the lump in her throat.

She hesitated and took a deep breath to center herself.

"Can't you still fly as long as you have another pilot with you?" Kate topped over her glass of syrah and took it to the table.

"I'm not flying with an instructor. That would be like putting training wheels back *on* — my independence gone. It's a badge of honor to be solo in the sky. Life's in your own hands. At least it used to be."

Ox dished up the lasagna with violent cuts against the noodles as though taking his frustration out on the food.

Kate sliced into the bread as the crust crunched under the weight of the knife. Bayou's eyes popped open, and his nose twitched.

"You know Bayou can still do his therapy, just on the ground." Kate brought her plate to the table.

Every day this week, Ox had needed his cane. Of course, he had bad and good days, but this last week had proved more brutal than usual. She helped out as much as she could with Bayou and the inn, but sometimes it exhausted her. Yet, Kate didn't know what could've happened that would've caused the doctor to ground him. It all seemed as sudden as a tablecloth magic trick. *Are things worse than Ox led me to believe?*

Kate couldn't bring herself to flat out ask Ox. Besides, he would tell her if he wanted to. And she couldn't point fingers when she kept things to herself, like the vacancy in her heart about not having children.

They'd discussed kids before they married. And while neither of them had changed their minds, emptiness remained in their home. She worked through those emotions, at least she thought and turned her focus on getting a sibling for Bayou. However, Ox deflected any conversation about a new member of the Swanson bunch, always saying they could discuss it later.

"Flying is a huge part of my life, and now it's gone." He picked up his fork and set it back down as he rested his head into his left hand. "I hate this disease."

"I hate it too." Kate reached for his hand and set hers on top of his. "You sounded like you had something else to say earlier."

"It was nothing." He waved her off with his fork.

She didn't want to remind him of all the things he could still do because that didn't fix his current reality.

Bayou let out a loud sigh that filled the silent kitchen, causing Ox to laugh. His body shook with deep laughter. The kind of rolling laugh that's contagious. Kate began laughing so hard she gasped to find her breath.

The dog's sigh was a blatant attempt to remind them that he was indeed sitting there without any of the scraps he so desperately needed before all one hundred and fifteen pounds of him wasted away.

She pinched her eyes closed, grateful for at least a few seconds of happiness on a day full of disappointment. If only Kate could laugh away those avoided questions.

Chapter 4

Today, Ox would spend the morning calling his clients to let them know he and Bayou would no longer provide their flying therapy classes.

He looked around his office filled with airplane photography and located his favorite one, a picture of Bayou sitting on the back bench of his Cessna. Kate had snapped the photo during the fateful January they'd helped her with her flying anxiety.

Ox always feared this day would come if the MS progressed or the medication didn't work as it should, but this was far sooner than he'd planned.

His heart pounded wildly, and waves of nausea rose in his throat whenever he imagined the day he'd have to sell his plane. Today, the thought of it caused his right cheek to twitch. He pressed his fingers into it, rubbing it in a circular motion trying to make it stop.

Snoring loudly, Bayou rested on his bed in the corner of the office, but not so loud that Ox couldn't hear his thoughts driving him nuts.

His eyes paused on a photo of their honeymoon, and last night's dinner flooded back to his mind. How close he'd come to letting his emotions get the best of him. Thankfully, he stopped himself before the words "why I didn't want to get married" slid out like an evil snake's tongue.

And in his moment of anger, he would've meant it, even if it shattered both their hearts. He hoped it was a passing emotion; however, when he looked at Kate this morning, he knew those words were true. She deserved the best. It was apparent he could no longer be what he promised when they said their vows.

But for now, he focused on the task at hand. He couldn't talk with Kate until their friends were gone. The last thing he wanted to do was ruin their visit or Maggie's wedding.

Taking a long breath, Ox dialed the number to his client, Victoria, from the inn's landline phone.

Gripping the receiver, it occurred to him, maybe someday phone companies would no longer support landlines. Perhaps he had no control over anything.

"Hello," said Victoria.

"Hi, Victoria, it's Ox." He glanced at the photo on his desk of Kate, Bayou, and him standing in front of his Cessna, their sunglasses shielding their eyes from the light.

"Ox, how are you?" she chimed.

"I have some unfortunate news."

Victoria was silent.

He shut his eyes. "I'm going to have to cancel our next appointment, and I won't be able to reschedule. I won't be flying anymore."

There, he'd said it, and it was as horrible as he'd imagined. Ox ran his hand through his hair as he kept a tight grip on the phone.

"Ox," Victoria said, "I completely understand."

"You . . . you, do?"

"As you know, my husband's sister has MS, and she's learned to modify her life because she also had to give up some of her favorite things. I'm sorry to hear you are too."

"Thank you," Ox mumbled. What else could he say?

Bayou sprang up on his dog bed and took his back leg to his ear, scratching it frantically. Ox waved his hand to get the dog's attention, but he kept right on thumping his paw against his ear.

"But I won't be stopping the therapy sessions," Victoria said.

Ox blinked hard, trying to focus on the phone call.

The dog's back pressed against the wall causing the picture frames to shake and tilt with each flick his paw made to his ear.

"I'm sorry, Victoria, I won't be able to take you up in the plane anymore. Ever again." Ox waved a hand at Bayou as the thumping continued. "My neurologist has grounded me."

"I understand, but unless he grounded you to your room, I still need Bayou's services. Can we keep the same time and day for our therapy?"

Bayou flopped down and rubbed his ear against the bed.

"I . . . I guess?" Ox shook his head in confusion.

"Perfect. I'll see you later this afternoon then, bye."

"Bye," he replied, but Victoria had already hung up.

Ox pulled the phone away from his ear and inspected it before setting it back onto the charging base. "No part of this week has gone as expected."

A thunderous thump echoed down the hall, and Ox shuffled out of his office, cane in hand, with Bayou gaining from behind.

"I'm okay." Kate pushed her wild curls out of her face.

In the living room, on her knees, his wife was surrounded by a scattered pile of hardcover books. "I tried to stack them so I could dust behind them without having to take them all down. They sort of fell."

"Why are you dusting? You should be relaxing while you still can."

"I could do a lot of things, like eat three ice cream sandwiches and drink wine at nine in the morning, but I didn't because I'm an adult with many responsibilities."

Thanks for reminding me I'm one of them.

He stepped down into the living room. "The oddest thing happened when I called Victoria."

"Oh yeah?" Kate glanced up, stacking the books in her arms.

Numbness tingled in his right fingers, and he switched the cane to his left hand. Ox flexed it as though doing so would make it better.

"She still wants to use Bayou for therapy and told me to come over to her place at our scheduled therapy time."

Kate stood up, her chin resting on the stack of books in her arms. She set the books back on the now dusted shelf that surrounded the fireplace. "That's promising. Do you know what she has in mind?"

"It caught me off guard, and I didn't think to ask. I guess I'll find out." He watched as Bayou leaned back into a sloppy-sit and shook his head a few times. "Are you heading out soon to pick up Ali and Matt?"

"Ali's flight gets in first, so I thought we'd have lunch at Larry's while we wait for Matt's plane to land. That way I'm not driving back and forth to the inn."

"Sounds like a good plan with Larry's being close to the airport." Ox approached Bayou and flipped up his right ear between his fingers. Then he checked the dog's left ear. "Well, it's reddish-brown; I think he has an ear infection."

With the e-a-r word, the dog's eyes dilated, and he bolted from the room as though being chased by a dognapper.

"Before you go, can you help me get his ear drops in?" Ox headed to the hall closet and gathered the ear cleaner along with two cotton balls.

He followed Kate into the master bedroom, where she'd cornered Bayou near the window.

With her hands wrapped around him, Kate stood over him like he was a quarter-operated miniature horse ride outside the grocery store. "I know, buddy, but we need to give you medicine."

Together they blocked Bayou's escape and team-worked the situation, getting the drops in each ear and wiping it with the cotton ball. Once finished, the dog darted around the room, diving and rubbing his head left and right on every surface he located, trying to free the drops from his ears.

"You'd think he would handle this better by now," Kate huffed, placing her hands on her hips.

"You'd think." Ox closed the lid on the cleaner. "He's too smart for *our* own good. But, back on topic, I know it's been difficult not being able to spend time with Ali."

"Emails and an occasional phone call are not the same. The last time I saw Ali was at our wedding. That seems like it was forever ago."

"Both of your lives changed at nearly the same time, but lucky for me, I won." Ox pushed a smile upon his face, no matter how hard it was to be anything but depressed, being aware of the inevitable.

Kate blushed, and she took a few steps toward him and puckered her lips, overly dramatic, and he kissed them. "I think I won."

He hugged her close and wished every muscle in his body could keep from pushing her out of his life. It was unthinkable to drag her down with him. And he hoped he could find a way to get her to understand she needed to do what was best for her and not for him.

Chapter 5

Kate parked her navy blue 4Runner in the Crooked River Airport parking lot and made her way to the main doors.

A solid layer of clouds coated the underside of the sky, creating temperatures in the mid-fifties and sticky humid air. The smell of jet fuel caused her to lightly cough as she stepped closer to the main entrance.

She snickered, thinking about what the high in Phoenix would be today, at least one-hundred and ten.

The airport doors slid open, and she entered, going to her left. She couldn't go too far inside due to the security measures, but she'd be able to wait in the baggage claim area for her best friend.

Memories of her first time meeting Ox, spotting him with his face behind a book, filtered through her mind like a beloved slide show. She'd had a disastrous morning, and he'd made it better almost instantly, even if his welcome had been a bit sarcastic. And although Ox was going through a life-changing and challenging time, she wouldn't trade one second of it to be with anyone else. She loved him so much, sometimes it hurt.

A group of people merged into the baggage claim area, and Kate stretched up onto her tippy-toes to try and spot her best friend.

She didn't expect Ali to look much different than the last time she'd seen her. They'd shared enough photos via text messages and social media to know not much changed in their appearance except for longer hair and the start of a few wrinkles.

On her tippy-toes, Kate spotted the familiar sleek licorice black hair and called out, "Ali!"

She gave a few jumps to try and see the rest of the woman's face. Then, excitement to hug her best friend caused her hands to wave frantically in the air. "Ali!"

"Kate," Ali declared, breaking through the crowd. "Scene, Kate. Why must you always make a scene?"

Kate hugged her best friend with little jumps of joy, and then she pushed Ali to arm's length. "Don't be too happy to see me."

Ali provided a closed-mouth smile. "You know I'm the over-excited one about everything."

Kate squinted. "Your jokes aren't any better."

Ali's hair might be longer; however, her way of dressing hadn't changed—always fancier than what was needed. Today she had on black high-waisted paperbag ankle pants, a white linen button-up top, and strappy sandals. In addition, Ali had enough bracelets on her right wrist to make a pirate jealous.

"Are you taller?" Ali squeezed Kate's shoulders.

"Most definitely not." Kate laughed.

"I guess I'm used to shorter people in Shanghai. I always felt like a giant walking the streets."

"Are you hungry?" Kate adjusted her purse on her shoulder. "I thought we could head over to Larry's. Matt's flight won't land for another two hours, and I'd hate to drive back home only to turn around."

"Let's eat. I'm famished. I slept the entire flight from Pudong to Seattle and didn't so much as get something to drink. And the flight from SeaTac here is so short they don't offer anything." Ali touched her face, showing off her manicured coral pink nails. "My complexion must be horrid."

"Nothing a little greasy food won't fix."

After waiting for Ali's two pieces of matching black luggage with red zippers, they loaded up Kate's 4Runner and headed down the road to Larry's.

"Are you happy to be back?" Kate opened the restaurant's front door to the scent of grilled beef and the chattering of diners scraping silverware on plates.

"Well, it's rainy, humid, and hot in Shanghai right now, so at least it's not hot here." Ali smiled.

"And it's not raining today."

Faye wasn't in her usual spot to welcome guests; in her place was a teenage boy with a buzz cut.

"Welcome to Larry's. Table for . . . ?"

"Just us two." Kate beamed, unsure if it was in anticipation of something to eat, her best friend being home, or the mixture of the two.

"Right this way." The unenthusiastic teenager pointed with the menus.

They followed the host to their booth, and Kate spotted Faye at a table near the back and gave a quick wave.

"Your server will be right with you." The teenager set the two menus opposite each other on the table and left before they sat down.

Kate and Ali shimmed into the booth but didn't bother to pick up the menus.

"I wanted to tell you in person . . . " Ali rearranged the silverware on top of the white paper napkin.

"Right to the point, well, this doesn't sound good." Kate weaved her fingers together and set them in front of her on the table.

Ali tucked a sleek section of hair behind her ear and adjusted her posture. "My position at the company in Shanghai was eliminated."

Kate's stomach sank. "Are you serious?"

The month of July had some serious explaining to do if it didn't turn around, and soon.

"Sadly, yes. At this point, I'm not sure what I'm going to do outside of continuing to apply for jobs. I packed up my apartment and had everything shipped to a storage facility in Seattle."

"But," Kate muttered, "but, when? Why?"

A glare reflected off the laminated tabletop, and Kate reached up to adjust the window's blinds. "I don't understand; why didn't you say anything? You said you were coming here to visit and take a vacation. Not looking for work and a place to live."

"I didn't lie. I'm here on vacation. Only now, it might be for a tad bit longer than planned. Don't worry, I booked an Airbnb for after my time is up at the inn."

Kate pressed her arms into the edge of the table, indenting her skin. "I feel horrible. Had I known, we could've saved your room for longer. It's our busy season. We're fully booked for the rest of the year. And now with Ox's bad news and Maggie's wedding."

"Bad news?" Ali inspected the flatware. "What wedding?"

"Girls!" Faye approached the table, her crimson apron worn and faded at the pockets. "Ali, so great to see you."

Faye reached into the booth and gave Ali a quick side hug, which she accepted with some restraint. "How have you been?"

"Good." Ali half-smiled and readjusted her shirt.

Kate knew darn well Ali wouldn't be blabbing about her current unemployment. She'd never divulge more than was needed until the occasion arose. Even in college, getting information from her was like trying to pull teeth from a closed mouth.

"Do you girls know what you want?" Faye put her hands on her hips.

"Cheeseburger," Ali said, "with extra avocado, fries, and a Coke with lime."

"I'll have a Sloppy Larry's, sweet potato fries, and a Coke with lemon." Kate handed the menus to Faye. "Thank you."

She tapped the back of the menus, smiled, and headed toward the kitchen's order window behind the bar.

"You'd be surprised how hard it is to find avocados in Shanghai." Ali crossed her arms and leaned back into the booth.

"You can't ignore the issue with deflection. What's your plan? I know you made a list."

"I plan to eat my weight in avocados in the next few weeks."

Kate tilted her head. "Not *that* plan."

"Shanghai was an adventure, and I loved all of it, but I'm ready for a change of scenery. I'm ready for a new adventure. I just don't know what yet. The company gave me a nice severance package. Thankfully, that'll allow me time to look for something else before I end up taking cold showers and eating ninety-nine-cent bread."

"Good luck finding bread *that* cheap."

Ali sneered and picked at the underside of her pointer fingernail. "I decided to throw the net wide and applied for positions all over the globe. You know me, never one to stay in the same spot."

"What exactly does all over the globe mean?" Kate flicked her hands out.

"From top to bottom." Ali leaned forward, bringing her chin close to her hands. "Or is it side to side?"

"But you must have a plan."

"Yes, and my plan is based on what I catch when my net lands."

"What if your net snags on something?" Kate watched a group of construction workers enter the restaurant.

"Not possible. If a plan is solid, as mine is, then there's no reason to worry about a snag."

Kate had hoped living in Shanghai had changed Ali, but it was now clear that her best friend was still trying to avoid being truly happy and finding love.

Chapter 6

Ox enjoyed the pleasant drive to Victoria's home. Hundred-year-old evergreens flanked the sides of the road to her house that started about a mile off the paved street. Since the sun didn't reach the tire tracks, rainwater rarely dried in the puddles on the packed down dirt road.

Ox parked off in the sparse gravel and opened his truck's back door for Bayou to jump out.

Victoria's home, built of deep rich amber-colored logs, nestled itself into a little gap of trees. Pansies in yellow and purple bloomed in mismatched pots littering the patio.

He knocked on the front door adorned with a flower-patterned glass oval in the center.

Bayou sat nicely while Ox gripped his cane and leaned on it. His legs were weak, and he needed to sit down as soon as possible.

The door eased opened, and Victoria emerged from behind it, dressed in a Christmas-themed T-shirt and jeans.

"Hi." Ox pointed at Victoria. "Out of clean clothes?"

She looked down, stretched her shirt in her hand, and laughed. "No, it's July. An acceptable time to wear Christmas stuff. It's not like I can wear a T-shirt in December. I'd freeze." Victoria stepped back and waved him inside.

"I'm sorry about having to cancel the flying therapy." Ox was slow and methodical with his steps. "Do you mind if I sit?"

"Oh, yes, please." Victoria directed them into the living room right off the entryway.

A woman about the same age as Victoria sat on one of the two plump stone-blue couches opposite each other with a wrought iron coffee table in the middle. Off to the side of the room was a stone fireplace.

"Ox, this is my sister, Leslie. Leslie, this is Ox and Bayou."

Leslie stood up and stretched out her hand, shaking his. Then she looked at Bayou, and the dog raised his paw in the air.

"He'd like to shake your hand, too," Victoria stated.

The sister leaned forward and grinned at the dog. "Nice to meet you, Bayou." She took his paw in her hand for a few seconds and then let go. "I've heard a lot about you from Victoria."

With the help of his cane, Ox lowered himself onto the couch across from the women. "I think more people know my dog than me."

Bayou laid down at Ox's feet but focused on Leslie, who sat rigid on the couch.

Victoria sat next to Leslie and pressed her elbows on her knees. "The reason why I asked to keep the therapy appointment is for Leslie. Unfortunately, she's been diagnosed with cancer, and the doctor suggested she spends time with a therapy dog before and during her chemotherapy sessions to help with any anxiety."

Ox reached down and petted Bayou's head. Just the mention of doctors made him uneasy. "He doesn't have any training in a medical setting."

A twinge of guilt coursed through him. It wasn't that he didn't want to help, but he couldn't do, with or without Bayou. And he didn't want to see if he could overcome it; the challenge was too personal.

"He doesn't need it." Victoria clasped her hands together. "Bayou's a therapy dog for anxiety, and that's precisely what my sister is dealing with."

"I guess I can't speak for myself." Leslie crossed her arms and slumped forward.

Victoria turned to her sister. "Les, you know I only want to help."

"Ox, do you think Bayou can help me?" Leslie shifted and stretched her hand toward his dog.

Bayou eased up on all fours and used his nose to guide himself closer to Leslie. He sniffed her hand as though it was the first time meeting her and quickly gave the top of it a lick which caused her to laugh.

"That tickles." Leslie moved her hand to the dog's head, running it down behind his ear.

Ox twisted his cane back and forth between his fingers. "Yes, what Victoria said is true. The logistics behind anxiety would be the same. Anxiety, being a reaction where you feel excessive nervousness, apprehension, and fear based on your location externally or internally. So, if it's a plane, hospital, or fear of heights, your location is causing your anxiety. It's the same stepping into the medical building as stepping onto my plane."

"You're so sweet, Bayou," Leslie oozed, scratching the dog's chest as he kept his face close to hers.

"I feel horrible about cutting your therapy short, Victoria." Ox diverted from the conversation as his breathing grew ragged, thinking about the hospital. At least he assumed the chemotherapy would be at the hospital.

"I was almost done with my sessions and felt pretty good on our last one."

Ox forced a smile. "That's great."

Bayou returned, his nose touched Ox's hand resting on his knee. "Hey, buddy."

"Ox, I know your heart is wrapped up in flying, but I hope you and Bayou will be able to help my sister." Victoria folded her hands and placed them in her lap. "Bayou is simply the best. Don't prevent his abilities from ending."

Ox took a deep breath and looked at Victoria and then Leslie. "Of course, Victoria. Bayou still has years of service left in him to make a difference."

Victoria's mouth fell at the edges, and her eyes saddened as they lowered. "I'm sorry, Ox, I didn't mean it like that."

Ox stood unsteady as he gripped his cane. "I can't do this. Bayou, he can't do this."

He needed a nap. He needed not to have MS.

"Please, Ox, I know this is not easy." Victoria made her way over to him, picked up Bayou's leash, and handed it to Ox. "Because of you and Bayou, I'm going to be able to fly with my husband for our vacation. An actual vacation we planned but were never able to do because of my anxiety. Bayou has made it possible, and you did too. It's not just about the dog; it's about the owner." She glanced over her shoulder. "My sister needs this."

"I understand," Ox mumbled, disappointed he'd let his emotions show in front of anyone.

He made his way, with Bayou at his side, to the front door. When he opened it, he turned around and looked back into the living room. Leslie remained seated on the couch, focusing on her hands, and then wiped a finger under her eye.

"I'm sorry." Ox stepped onto the porch.

"Ox," Victoria called out, but he didn't turn around. "Ox, think about it, please."

By the time Ox pulled into the Cessna's hangar at the airport, Bayou was whining. Ox had driven in a back way, hoping to avoid running into his wife. It was nearing the time that Matt's plane would land, and the last thing Ox wanted was Kate seeing the despair on his face.

"I know, buddy, I feel the same way." He climbed from the driver's seat, and before Ox could open the back door all the way, Bayou had jumped down.

The mid-day sunlight filtered through the open hangar and bounced off the plane. Ox popped the Cessna's door, and Bayou rested his paws on the little bit of available floorboard.

Leaning his cane against the Cessna frame, he attempted to hoist Bayou up, but he could only get the dog halfway there. Bayou's front paws clawed at the floor, desperate to get himself inside. The dog's head weaved back and forth with his attempts.

Once Bayou was all the way in the Cessna, Ox held tight to the door's frame, his arms ached with fatigue. He sighed, unsure if he had enough energy to hoist himself into the seat.

"When did this get so high?" He placed his hands on the seat's bottom.

Bayou sat in the passenger seat, looking forward as though he was ready to fly the plane himself.

"Can I get you a headset?" Ox leaned onto his elbows. "Don't watch, buddy. This isn't going to be pretty."

Ox grabbed hold of the far side of the seat, where the seat belt clipped in. He set one foot on the landing gear and wedged the other foot into the frame as he heaved himself forward. His cane clapped on the concrete as he launched his body forward and yanked himself upright and onto the seat.

"I almost pulled a Kate."

Moving his hand over the yoke, Ox closed his eyes. Without looking, he knew every inch of the cabin. He kept his eyes shut as he focused on his breathing. Memories of his first flying lesson and later his first solo trip flashed through his mind.

Without opening his eyes, he reached for his headset and slid it on. The sound of Bayou's tail thumped slightly on the seat. But when Ox drew his eyes open, he noticed his dog was looking out the passenger window towards the hangar's entrance door. And Ox knew Bayou was waiting for someone to arrive.

"Sorry, Bayou, it's just us." Ox petted his dog's head.

The dog let out a whimper and attempted to turn his body around as he looked out the rear of the plane.

"All you want to do is help people," Ox mumbled into the silent headset.

He slid the headsets from his ears to around his neck as he stared off through the cockpit windows one final time.

Chapter 7

Kate hurried across the airport's parking lot, heading, once again, for the main entrance. She was running late, literally, and when she made her way through the sliding doors, she spotted Matt walking toward her.

"Matt!"

He paused, a single piece of luggage in hand. "Kate."

"I'm so sorry I'm late." She hugged him.

"I thought maybe I got the message confused on my end and was supposed to meet you outside."

Matt's attire was as snappy as it was on his last visit. He wore boat shoes, khakis, and a striped polo shirt. His raven black hair was longer on the sides, nearly covering his stud earring. And he'd gone lighter on the gel, so he didn't look like he was auditioning for *Grease 3*.

"Ali and I lost track of time." Kate squeezed the keys in her hand. "And, no, you're not confused, I said inside. It's my fault. My mind has been elsewhere lately."

"Ali, is . . . with you?" Matt's eyes narrowed. "I mean, I know she's here, this week I . . . I mean, she's here in the car or back at the inn?"

Kate's brow furrowed. "She's in the 4Runner."

Matt glanced at the parking lot and back at Kate. "Is my zit noticeable?" He pointed at his nose. "I feel like Rudolph."

She pulled her top lip down with her bottom teeth, containing her laughter. "A zit?"

Matt set his luggage at his shoes. "I'm too old to get them. But there it is, flashing like a warning light."

Kate leaned close, examining his nose. "Well, I can see it, but if you hadn't pointed it out, I doubt I would've noticed it."

She winced because her statement wasn't entirely true. The zit was noticeable without being alerted to it, but she didn't want Matt to stress out about it.

"I don't want Ali's first in-person impression of me to . . . to be a red neon bulb."

"You mean you didn't post on social media for her and everyone else to see?" Kate chuckled. "No one cares. Now, guide the way with your light." Kate hoped he could see the humor in it and realize his overreaction.

Matt groaned and lifted his suitcase while Kate shook her head.

"Good to see you haven't changed," she mumbled.

"You don't have any makeup in your purse, do you?" Matt asked as they weaved through the parked cars.

"Don't turn my way; you're blinding me." Kate held her hand up, shielding her eyes.

"I'm glad you find my zit humorous."

"I do. Oh, I'm parked over to the left, the 4Runner." Kate pointed a row over.

Matt halted. "Which one? There are three other 4Runners over there."

"The navy blue one."

As they approached, Kate hit the hatch release for the back and lifted it up. The passenger door popped open, and Ali stepped out.

"Matt, great to meet you." She held out her hand. "In real life."

"Matt." The words tumbled from his lips as though he was unsure of himself. "I'm Matt."

Kate leaned around the back end of the 4Runner as he stuck his right hand out for a shake and used his left hand to act like he had an itch on his nose.

"I have some great toner you can use to clear up that zit." Ali pointed.

Matt peered over his shoulder at Kate as his eyes widened. With a jerk, he turned to open the back door and climbed in, shutting the door harder than needed. Ali shrugged her shoulders at Kate.

"So, Matt," Kate said, sliding into the driver's seat, "we're excited you're here, but Ox wanted to make sure you knew the inn still doesn't have any fancy coffee."

"I doubt we'll be snowed in this time. I can run out and get some," Matt said from the back seat.

"Fancy coffee?" Ali lowered her square-framed sunglasses to the bridge of her nose. "You mean normal coffee? How normal people drink coffee? I think I'll have to join Matt on his coffee run."

As Kate started the 4Runner, she didn't need to look in her rearview mirror to know Matt was grinning.

Chapter 8

Ali stood in the living room, her eyes fixated on the view out the massive windows. "I'm delighted to finally get to spend time here."

Ox had missed the first part of what Ali said as he debated letting Bayou partake in therapy for Leslie. Victoria had emailed him the information with a message hoping he'd reconsider. Reading through it, he'd been optimistic that the chemo treatments were at one of those centers he'd seen on television, or at least at the doctor's office. Instead, as suspected, Leslie's chemo took place at the local hospital.

Bayou laid on the floor and sprung up anytime anyone moved. Ox worried that without the days of therapy, the dog would soon grow bored.

"We're glad you're finally able to be here too, Ali." Ox adjusted the couch's pillow behind his back for more support. "Nice zit, Matt."

Matt's hand went to his nose and his face flushed.

"There's a Fourth of July celebration I thought we could attend in town," Kate mentioned. "They usually have some amazing food trucks, music, and local goodies to purchase. Last year, I had my photography displayed there. But this season, I've been so busy working on a new project that I decided to skip it."

"I remember how fun those were when Kate and I were teenagers," Ali stated and turned to look at the group.

Matt stood opposite Ali. "Sounds like a good plan to me."

"Ox, do you think you're up for it?" Kate asked.

He hated to openly admit it in front of others when he was having a difficult day. "I'm not sure. I need to get a few things done first."

Ox knew Kate would understand what he was getting at because he always made time for her. So when he mentioned he had things to do, it was his way of letting her know, when others were around, that he was having a rough day.

Kate handed over two iron skeleton keys for their guests' rooms. "Matt and Ali, why don't you get settled into your rooms. I'm going to help Ox with a few things. We can leave about five." She reached out her hand to her husband.

Ox used it, along with his cane, and rose from the couch. Feeling Ali and Matt's eyes focused on him, he hoped Bayou would do something, anything to draw the attention off him.

With a glance, Ox raised his eyes at Bayou as if a secret command only they understood. The dog moved in front of Ali and Matt, flopped to the floor, rolled over, and kicked all four paws into the air.

"Good boy," Ox mentioned leaving the room. "Show them your break-dance moves."

As he made his way to the bedroom, his wife followed. "I'll be okay. I just need a nap."

Once he sat on the bed, she kissed above the stubble on his right cheek. She joined him on the edge of the mattress and placed her hand on his thigh.

"You know I've been thinking about Bayou and the—" she bit her lip, "—his lack of activity, and I'd hate to see him get lonely."

"What are you getting at?" Ox rubbed his right eye with his knuckle.

"It might be nice for him to have a playmate."

"I thought we decided we won't be having kids, not with my MS."

"We did." She giggled. "But that's not —"

"I'm tired. Can we talk about this later?" Ox adjusted his pillow, punching it with his hand. *Why does she find it funny?*

"Sure, I'm sorry for bringing it up." She stood halfway, and without a kiss goodbye, hurried to the door, softly shutting it behind her as she left.

He fought off sleep as he thought about Kate's mention of Bayou needing a sibling and the email from Victoria, both weighing heavier than he wanted at the moment.

In the past, they'd discussed a baby at length. They'd gone over it, and the decision was final. Why would she be changing her mind now that he could no longer fly? He didn't need to fill a void or replace flying with something. Why had Kate decided now that she'd spring a change of heart about a baby on him? Did she suddenly think they could raise a child, take care of him, Bayou, and the inn?

Maybe she'd seen a baby when she was at the airport. His eyes drifted shut as he continued to debate. Had she realized their marriage was no longer enough for her? Perhaps the end of *them* was going to be easy for Kate.

Chapter 9

When Kate returned to the living room, she paused and hung back behind the wall, sneaking a peek of Ali and Matt. She already knew by Matt's horrible zit-hindered introduction with Ali that he found her to be, at the very least, charming.

The pair was still in the living room, on their knees, taking turns rubbing Bayou's belly. The dog's tail swished back and forth on the rug showing his delight.

Matt kept one hand near his nose, but his vision was stuck on Ali. A dorky smile creased his lips. Yet Kate knew her best friend well enough to know it'd take a lot more than a smile to catch her attention.

A knock at the door caused Kate to forgo any more spying.

She hurried into the entryway, trying to make it look like she'd not just been standing behind the hall.

Grabbing the knob, she swung open the door, unsure who it could be as they weren't expecting any guests. "Maggie."

"I'm sorry to come over without calling, but I was on my way to the grocery store and wanted to see if you had a few minutes to discuss the wedding?"

Kate motioned Maggie in. "Of course, however, Ox is resting, and Ali and Matt are here."

"That's okay, but I hope I didn't wake him." Maggie made her way inside and eyed the living room. "Hello."

Kate shut the front door. "No, Ox is a heavy sleeper."

"It's been a long time," Matt stated, rising from the floor.

Bayou flipped over onto all fours and trotted over to greet Maggie.

"It sure seems that way. Hi, Matt." Maggie gave the dog a pet before turning to Ali. "Hi, I think we met for maybe half a second last time you were here. I'm Maggie."

Ali stood up straight and walked over, her hand extended for a shake. "Nice to see you again."

"Great to see you both." Maggie smiled. "I'm not sure if Kate mentioned it, but you're both invited to the wedding."

"Kate told us about the engagement. Congratulations." Ali attempted to brush off Bayou's fur that clung to her pants.

"Thank you. It's nice knowing the wedding will be in just a few days instead of having to wait for six months," Maggie said.

"Will you and Richard be attending the Fourth of July celebration tonight?" Kate asked as they moved toward the kitchen.

"Richard's hip has been bugging him the last few days, so we're going to skip it." Maggie removed her purse from her shoulder and set it on the kitchen table. She pulled out a small black and green striped notebook.

Kate moved to the junk drawer at the island and produced a pen and notepad. "I'm ready." She wiggled the pad in the air and pulled out a chair next to Maggie.

"If you'll excuse me," Ali stated. "I'm going to head up to my room. Come get me when we're ready to head out."

Kate nodded.

"Me too," Matt added and followed Ali up the stairs to their rooms, which were situated next door to each other.

Bayou tilted his head, watching them disappear before positioning himself at the foot of the table.

"Do I sense a hint of romance in the air between those two?" Maggie leaned over her notebook.

"I have my fingers crossed for a love match," Kate stated through clenched teeth. "Before I let this become reality television vibey, we must discuss your wedding."

"We want to say our vows at sunset, on the back patio. I know it'll be late since the sun doesn't set until around nine. I'll be too nervous to eat, but I figured everyone else will be famished. So, maybe some great wine and a simple meal, then we'll exchange vows and wrap it all up with cake and coffee. I know it's not the traditional flow of a wedding."

"It's your second chance love." Kate reached out and squeezed the top of Maggie's hand. "You should do it any way you want."

Maggie took her other hand and set it on top of Kate's. "I wanted to see if you'd be my maid of honor?"

Kate allowed her pen to fall onto the notepad below. "Maggie, I'd be honored to be your maid of, well, honor." A giggle escaped as she pressed her lips together in a smile.

"Wonderful. And please wear any dress you'd like. No point in spending money on some bridesmaid dress you'll hate or never wear again."

"I think I have the perfect dress in my closet. How many people do you plan on inviting?" Kate asked.

"There'll be you, Ox, Ali, and Matt. Bayou, of course. Richard's invited his two boys, but they live in Virginia and didn't seem interested in watching their father re-marry. However, I invited my sister." Maggie squeezed the notepad as her knuckles turned white. "We're not close anymore, my sister and I. It's doubtful she'll show up. Yet, I figured it was a good opportunity to see each other."

"Well, if she does show up, we'll make room for her." Kate scribbled more notes down. "What are you thinking of for snacks and wine?"

"I was hoping Ox could make his famous summer pasta. It's such a light dish and a perfect match with the wine. Richard and I picked up some nice bottles the last time we were in Sequim at the Wind Rose Cellars."

"Perfect. What about the cake?"

"River Bakery is making us a two-tiered blueberry lemon cake. They use local blueberries."

Kate's mouth watered. "I want a piece of that cake right now."

Maggie laughed. "Trust me. The sample was not big enough."

Kate tapped her pen on the pad. "Flowers?"

"You always have such beautiful hydrangeas. Would you mind doing a few centerpieces for the outside tables and maybe the table where the cake and food will be?"

"I'll put together vases of them in all the right places." Kate scribbled onto the notepad. "Oh, what about a bouquet?"

"Can you make me one? Or am I asking too much?"

"I'd love to make you one." Kate tapped her pen across her fingers. "Flowers, cake, food, wine, are we missing anything? Oh, music."

"Yes, we'd love to have some classics, Frank and Elvis. And photographs of the event."

"How could I forget that?"

"They might revoke your photography license. Good thing you don't need one." Maggie winked.

"Thank goodness because they might've pulled it when I fell backward off the dock last summer trying to capture Marina Days for this travel website and ruined my camera."

"I have complete faith in your skills, but maybe look behind you before you take any steps backward." Maggie rose from the chair. "I hope this is not too much to ask of you and Ox."

"It's our pleasure to be a part of your wedding."

"I can't thank you enough." She embraced Kate. "You're like the daughter I never had." Maggie pushed Kate's curly hair back over her shoulders.

A smile warmed Kate's cheeks.

"Should I invite your parents to the wedding?"

"Goodness, no." Kate shook her head. "My dad would complain under his breath about waiting for dessert, and my mom would fuss over everyone."

"Alright then, I guess that's it." Maggie clapped her hands, causing Bayou to snap his head up from his slumber. "We'll see you and everyone else on the big day, at seven p.m."

"Seven it is," Kate chimed.

"Tell Ox I said hi." Maggie grabbed her purse and slipped the notebook in it.

"I will. And have a nice cozy evening at home with Richard." Kate walked Maggie to the door. "Maybe you'll be able to see a few fireworks from the backyard."

"That would be nice. You know, I'm rather happy to stay home and not have to deal with the crowds."

"Sounds perfect." Kate pulled open the front door by the knob. "Bye, Maggie."

Maggie waved and made her way to her car as Kate closed the door. She took a deep breath, thinking about the wedding. It wouldn't be much work, but she worried about Ox and what kind of day he'd be having.

Kate pressed her pointer finger to her lip and pondered. She could do the flower arrangements, summer salad, and give the back patio a nice scrub down, which would leave Ox with nothing to do but rest.

She removed her cell phone from her back pocket and checked the clock in the middle of the screen. There was still time to read a few more chapters in the new book she'd picked up from the library and feed Bayou his dinner before she had to get ready to leave.

Kate found Bayou had moved to the living room and spread out on the floor, warming himself in the sunshine streaming through the windows. She went over to him and squatted down. His eyes eased open, and he rolled to his back, stretching out.

"You'd love to have a little brother or sister, wouldn't you? Someone to keep you entertained and play tug with your toys." She rubbed his belly. "Your dad is acting like I'm asking for a baby instead of a puppy. I wonder why he's suddenly against it."

Standing, Kate put her hands on her hips and gazed down at Bayou. "Don't worry. I won't give up."

Chapter 10

The air smelled of summer warmth and smoked brisket as he and Kate made their way from the parking lot to the open field for the Fourth of July celebration.

Kate held Bayou's leash as Matt and Ali walked in front of them, the evening sky beginning its descent into night.

Thankfully, the nap had done Ox a little bit of good, but he still needed his cane for support. The last thing he wanted was to fall in front of everyone.

He squeezed Kate's hand as they weaved their way toward the booths lining the path to the food trucks. Although similar to the Winter Day held in January, this one didn't require a scarf and gloves to venture about, which suited Ox. The cold weather worsened his MS symptoms, stretching out the pain and muscle spasms like a rubber band about to snap.

Tonight's festivity stands offered everything from dried fruits and nuts to artists selling their paintings on canvases and woodworkers' trinkets. The booth directly to their right showcased a local winery, and a gloved worker handed out miniature sample cups.

Kate let Ox's hand go as she approached the booth and took a free sample. She turned back to her husband, motioning with a cup for him.

He shook his head no. "Enjoy it for me."

Matt and Ali both tried a sample of the white wine, while Kate stuck with the red blends.

"Ox?" A familiar voice came from behind him.

Shifting his gaze over his right shoulder, he found Victoria. "Hi."

"Great to see you here. Have you given any more thought to Bayou helping my sister?" Victoria asked.

Ox brought his hand to the back of his neck. "Where's Leslie? Is she not here?"

"She's with my husband getting food." Victoria pointed into the distance, where the scent of roasted meat filled the air with a smoky cloud.

"I meant to call you." Ox looked over at Bayou. "We look forward to working with Leslie."

As the words came from his mouth, he didn't feel any better about his fate, but he hoped it would bring something good to Leslie and Bayou's life.

"Ox." Victoria grabbed hold of his upper arm. "Thank you. Thank you so much."

She squeezed her eyes closed and then opened them, producing an elated smile. "I must tell Leslie the good news. After you left, she told me how much she enjoyed meeting Bayou. Thank you, Ox."

Victoria spotted Bayou and bent down, giving the dog a fast rub on his back. "Thank you, Bayou."

Victoria stood and brought her hands together. "Thank you, thank you."

Ox nodded and forced a smile as Victoria hurried off through the crowd.

"What was that about?" Kate stood in front of Ox, balancing two sample cups of wine in one palm and Bayou's leash in the other.

"I let Victoria know Bayou would be her sister's therapy dog for the chemo treatments." Ox adjusted his grip on the cane.

"Babe, that's great news. Bayou is going to do great." She stood on her tiptoes and kissed his cheek. "So are you. And this wine is good. We'll have to pick up a bottle or two on the way back. I hate carrying things around." Kate turned to the booth. "Will you be here after the fireworks?"

The lady with clear disposable gloves nodded. "Yes, of course. Which one would you like me to set aside for you?"

Kate leaned over the table to examine the menu as Bayou stretched the leash, trying to get closer to Matt and Ali.

"Matt, can you please take Bayou for a second?" Kate held the loop of the leash toward him.

Matt looked at Bayou and then back at Kate as though she was asking him to hold a leash attached to a grizzly bear.

Kate waved the leash like a mini flag. "He doesn't bite."

Matt took a step towards Kate and reached his hand out.

"He doesn't *always* bite," Ox added.

Matt guffawed. "Nice try, of course, the big guy doesn't bite. He's as gentle as they come."

Bayou made his way between Matt and Ali as Kate tried another sample of wine.

Matt, facing Ox, held the leash while Bayou turned the other direction and spotted a child at the next booth. The dog's tail went rigid, and his ears folded back to listen better.

"Matt," Ox raised his voice, but it was too late.

With a single yank forward from Bayou, like a sled dog leader, Matt lost his balance. He stumbled backward and spun sideways. Bayou sniffed the kid, who must have been around three years old, as the leash wrapped around Matt's knees, and he continued to try and regain his balance.

Ali and Kate turned to watch the ordeal unfold as Ox moved toward Matt. Ox reached out for the leash as Matt landed on his bottom on the trampled grass, taking a table of handmade wooden blocks with him.

The blocks flew everywhere and bounced off the thick fur of Bayou's back as the rest scattered on the ground. Unaware of the trouble he had caused, Bayou kept sniffing at the boy's hands, causing the child to erupt with giggles.

"And I thought I was clumsy," Kate stated, taking the leash from Matt before Ox could.

"Are you okay?" Ali stretched both hands down at Matt, and he grabbed them, hoisting himself onto his feet.

Matt's face flushed like a cherry. "Yes, but I won't be getting a dog anytime soon." He brushed off the tiny bit of grass on his pants.

"I couldn't agree more." Ali looked at Kate and then at Ox. "Sorry, I'm sure Bayou is a nice companion, but all the fur, drool, and knocking over things, including people. They're a lot like mischievous children."

Kate laughed as she gently guided the dog away from the toddler. "Bayou is the best, fur and all. Though, I'm pretty sure he's ninety-percent fur."

When Kate glanced over her shoulder, Ox's heart fluttered like a butterfly. The way she still made him feel nervous from time to time reminded him he didn't deserve her.

With the dog's leash in hand, Kate returned to the winery's table and put in an order for a bottle of their sangiovese and pinot noir.

Kate rejoined the group and linked her arm around his, with Matt and Ali walking in front of them.

Ox noticed how close they were standing. Matt chatted with Ali as their shoulders were inches from touching with every step. Ali laughed at something Matt said, and Kate nudged Ox in the arm.

"Look at that. I knew they'd hit it off," she whispered.

"Even if they are — even if they like each other — they don't live in the same state."

"Husband of mine, have you not learned yet? Never say never."

Before they left the inn, his wife had divulged Ali's secret about losing her job and not returning to Shanghai.

"Okay then, maybe say maybe." Ox pressed his cane into the grass with each step.

Walking closer to the scent of smoked meat and spun sugar, Ox spotted it. And in less than three seconds, Kate did also.

"Puppies!" she squealed. "Ox, look, the rescue center's here."

"Kate." But before he could say anymore, his wife and Bayou were no longer by his side.

A small open-top crate held a chocolate Labrador puppy, about three months old, and two other crates held a fluffy white dog weighing about five pounds and a black and white Spaniel of some kind.

"Ox, isn't he just the cutest?" Kate oozed as Bayou sniffed the dogs' crates, his tail swishing left and right.

He nodded and gave a forced smile. Sure the puppy was cute. Adorable even, but he had to worry about Kate wanting a sibling for Bayou, not another dog. And most certainly not both.

She handed him Bayou's leash and reached in, picking up the hefty chocolate puppy. "Oh, you're a chunky monkey."

"Isn't he too big to be picked up?"

"Never." Kate beamed with joy. "It's like holding a toddler."

As she snuggled the puppy against her cheek, he couldn't help but smile at the scene. If only he could give her everything she wanted in life, he would.

Kate continued to be smitten with the puppy as Matt and Ali watched. Ox's stomach groaned as the scent of buttery corn on the cob waffled past his nose. He inched close enough to reach his hand out and pet the little chocolate's furry head. The puppy must've weighed at least twenty-five pounds, and he had no idea how Kate found the strength to keep holding him.

"You're a gorgeous little pup." The fur velvety soft under Ox's palm as though his numbness and tingling went away at the touch of it. "I'm surprised they have these dogs here with the fireworks tonight."

A volunteer at the table overheard him. "Thank you for your concern. We'll be closing up shop before they start. You understand dogs. You're a step ahead of the game." The volunteer pointed at Bayou. "And your yellow Lab is a sturdy one."

Sturdy? "Thanks? He's an English Labrador. Slightly stocker than your normal Lab. It's sort of like calling a horse a donkey or vice versa."

"Babe?" Kate raised her shoulders and nestled her face against the pup's furry body.

She didn't need to say anymore. Ox already knew the question. "I love you, and you know I love dogs, but right now isn't a good time. Especially after you brought up . . . " he sighed.

"Please let me know if you're interested in giving the little chocolate nugget a furever home," the volunteer said.

"Ox," Kate whined again, as though he'd just grounded her to her room for a week. "He needs a home. We can be his family. Bayou . . . "

As Ox looked down, her voice faded. "Sorry, Kate. I'm going to take Bayou and find some food."

It took a few pulls on the leash to tear Bayou away from the cages, and as they made their way to the food trucks, Ox couldn't help but pause and glance back at the rescue's booth.

Matt and Ali were catching up to him, but he could see Kate was still holding the puppy in her arms in the distance.

"Do you think I'm being too stubborn about not getting another dog?" Ox asked as they approached.

"You're asking the wrong guy." Matt held his hands up in defense. "I'm still dizzy from the Bayou-Go-Round."

Ali crossed her arms. "I know you have a lot going on with your MS, but you need to give a little. And if you haven't figured it out by now, in the end, Kate gets her way or gets injured trying."

Ox nodded with a chuckle. "Just the other day, I caught her climbing on the counter to get a mixing bowl that was out of reach. She nearly slipped and went flying off the counter. Can you imagine her *and* a puppy?"

Ali giggled. "Talk about *America's Funniest Home Videos*. Wait, is that still on?"

"You watched it as a kid?" Matt's head twisted toward Ali. "Me too."

"I think *Wipe Out* is pretty funny too," Ali added.

"I love that show," Matt nearly shouted. "Do you want to go grab something to eat? I saw Mac's Tacos a few over."

"I love Mexican food, and it's been a long time since I've had some. And they'll have fresh avocados."

Matt grinned and then pointed with his head in the direction of the food.

Ox watched as they walked off, stealing glances at each other along the way.

When he turned back around, Ox could barely make Kate out in the distance. But he didn't need to see her and the rescue puppy to know he'd broken her heart.

Chapter 11

After putting the chocolate Lab puppy back into the playpen, Kate decided she couldn't face Ox at the moment. The way he didn't even entertain the idea of a puppy made her rigid with anger. She twisted her upper body, trying to get the stiffness in it to relax after holding the heavy ball of fur.

Strolling between the booths, she stopped at a vendor selling homemade soap and brought a few bars to her nose. One smelled of lilacs and the other of vanilla and honey.

After handing over a ten-dollar bill, she placed the purchases in her purse and made her way toward the Ferris wheel, off to the left of the booths.

Without a line, Kate climbed right up onto the platform and sat in the middle of the basket's seat as the worker pulled the bar down, locking it into place.

As the wheel began its climb, she breathed through her nose and closed her eyes. The breeze rustled her curls and caused her to shiver. Once she became level with the nearby treetops, the air no longer smelled of food.

The wheel began its first descent, and she spotted a couple holding the puppy she'd been snuggling with only fifteen minutes ago at the rescue booth. It was like watching ice cream fall off a cone in slow motion. Kate needed to do her best to forget about the little guy.

With each go-around, she focused on how distant everything below appeared. How innocent the world looked when you could pinch it between your fingers. Like a blanket of snow makes everything perfect and silent even amid chaos. Seeing the world at this angle reminded her to be happy with what she had because, at any given moment, Ox's life could change for the worst. And as much as she loved him, she could never erase his MS. Kate needed to blanket their world with as much perfection as she could muster, no matter how badly she wanted some things to be different. And if Ox didn't want a puppy, then she'd have to get over that too.

The Ferris wheel came to a stop, and the worker raised the bar. Kate hurried off to find her husband and friends like a teenager on a mission.

Locating Ox, Matt, and Ali at a table near the end of the row, Kate gave a short wave. Matt and Ali had plates of food in front of them, but Ox didn't have anything. She weaved her way around the patron-filled tables.

"Why don't you have any food?" she asked Ox once she reached them. "Are you not hungry?"

"I am, but I was waiting for you." He looked up at her and raised his hand in her direction.

Kate took it, wrapping her fingers around his as she glanced around. "Teriyaki?"

Ox shook his head. "I'm not in the mood for it. Do you want some?"

"No." She stood on her tippy toes and glanced around some more. "Oh, what about Maine crab?"

"That's where the corn on the cob smell is coming from." Ox turned his chin toward the buttery scent. "Yes, that sounds good."

"Do you want a crab sandwich and some corn?" she asked, understanding he couldn't be up walking around.

He'd need his energy to stay for the fireworks.

"If you don't mind," Ox said.

She allowed their hands to separate but not before squeezing it. "I'll be right back."

When she returned, Matt and Ali were halfway through their Mexican meal, and Bayou had taken up a prime spot next to them in hopes of enriching his life through dropped food.

Kate set down her plate of deep-fried crab and tater tots and slid Ox's plate of corn on the cob and an overflowing crab sandwich in front of him. Then, she removed two classic-style glass soda pop bottles from her purse and placed them on the table.

"Made it in one trip." Kate lowered onto the bench next to Ox. "How's your food?" she asked Ali and Matt.

"It's great, but it could be because I haven't had it in so long." Ali wiped her mouth with a tan disposable napkin.

"It's almost as good as some meals I had on vacation in Texas," Matt added. "Food trucks have come a long way."

"How are you doing with your skiing bucket list?" Ox bit into his sandwich.

Matt scooped up the last of his refried beans with his plastic fork. "I only have a few left on the list: Wyoming, Montana, Maine, and New Hampshire. There was an opportunity for a job in Maine, but I didn't have enough experience at the time. I'd planned on checking those two off when I landed the job. Alas."

"So you're still in New York?" Ali took a sip of beer from her half-empty clear plastic cup, the white foam sticking to the sides.

"Yes, I love the buzz of the city, but the job in Maine would've meant traveling for work, which sort of excited me. I guess I'm always trying to find something that makes me hungry to achieve more." Matt set his fork down.

"I like that." Ali smiled at him as though he was the last man on Earth.

Kate knew Ali well enough to understand that her best friend always made a mental list for careers. And maybe she would add New York to it.

"Do you like your job?" Matt asked. "Shanghai must be an amazing place to work. They're very career-focused there."

Ali and Kate's eyes met. And while Ali was prideful, she wasn't a liar. So at least Kate didn't have to worry about slipping up anymore in front of Matt.

Ali brought the cup to her lips and drained a few ounces of beer. "I'm . . . " She arched her back and folded her hands together. "I'm looking for a new job. My position, well, they let me go."

Ali lifted the cup and finished the beer. "I'm stuck in Washington at the moment. Not stuck." She pointed her index finger in the air. "I'm searching. I'm trying to ground myself in what's realistic and what I want."

"Oh, no, I'm sorry to hear that." Matt sipped from his cup, the liquid a darker color than Ali's beer. "Would you ever consider moving to New York? I mean, if you loved living in Shanghai, I'd suspect you'd love the bustle of New York City."

"I wouldn't mind it, but I loved living in another country. It quickly grew on me. I put in for various jobs and have had a few virtual interviews so far. One of them is in Australia. We'll see what happens."

"Australia? What an adventure. You're inspiring," Matt declared, staring at Ali like she was a queen with a mesmerizing tiara. "I don't think I'd have the guts to do that."

Ali blushed. "You'd be surprised what you can do if you want to live life to the fullest."

"You're really something." Matt's eyebrow arched with infatuation.

"Is that a compliment or —?" Ali twisted her body toward him.

"A compliment." Matt smiled. "I'm looking forward to getting to know you better this week."

"Me too." Ali tilted her head as though shy of the statement.

Kate might not have been able to predict the outcome of Matt and Ali's relationship, but so far, it was working out just as planned.

Chapter 12

While Kate, Ali, and Matt were locating an excellent spot to watch the fireworks, Ox made an excuse that Bayou needed to potty.

With Bayou at his side, Ox walked as fast as possible. Their lumbering strides mirrored each other as the sun's descent past the horizon brought a chill to the air. However, he didn't have time to run back to the truck to get a sweater.

As Ox looked up, the stars revealed themselves, and he hoped the rescue organization hadn't already packed up and left. But, reaching the stand, he only spotted empty cages.

"The puppy, the chocolate one?" he asked as Bayou sniffed the grass. "The one my wife fell in love with, is it still available for adoption?"

"I'm sorry; a couple adopted him a little bit ago. Labs are always the first to go. Our other volunteer went with the family for a home visit." The remaining volunteer collapsed one of the empty crates.

"We do, on occasion, have returned adoptions, or sometimes the home visit doesn't go well. Once the excitement wears off, and the family realizes it's a lot of work or the fit isn't the best." The volunteer put his hands on his hips. "If you want, I can take down your information. Are you specifically looking for a younger dog?"

Ox didn't need to tell him a puppy might soften the blow when he gathered the strength to discuss a possible divorce. Even thinking of divorce caused nausea to rise in his stomach.

Focus. One thing at a time.

Of course, he knew older dogs were just as important to adopt, but Kate's heart was set on raising a younger dog. It would allow her to experience some of those motherly vibes.

"Yes, at this time, we're looking for a puppy." Ox peered down at Bayou.

The volunteer approached and knelt in front of Bayou. "You said your dog is an English Lab?"

"He has an English accent too."

The volunteer's eyes traveled up to Ox, going from perplexed to a chuckle. He stretched out his hand for Bayou to sniff. "I guess that chocolate puppy was also. When I was going through the paperwork for the couple who adopted him, he was listed as English."

"Usually puppies in shelters are mutts. What was his story?"

"Sad. The owner passed. He has two sisters and two other brothers, but they were already adopted. He's a bit more hyper than his siblings. It's a lot of work to take care of a half-grown puppy already set in his ways, let alone a hyper one."

"He didn't seem hyper to me." Ox rested his cane against his leg and ran his hand through his hair. "I've been lucky with Bayou. He's mellow."

"Mellow yellow." The volunteer laughed. "Sorry, that was rather nineteen seventies. I'm Brandon." He stood and held out his hand.

Ox reached out and shook it. "Ox."

"Nice to meet you, Ox. So, he does okay with the fireworks?"

"Yes, he doesn't seem to mind them. But he's a therapy dog, so he's had extensive training over the years, which helps."

"My mom has a therapy dog for her seizures." Brandon collapsed another crate. "Amazing to see them work. Dogs show such dedication and drive for their people."

"They're brilliant animals." Ox looked up at the darkened sky as though making a wish that he could turn back time to when Kate asked him about getting the puppy.

"Here, write down your information, and I'll give you a call if anything comes up." He handed Ox a pen and a card.

Ox scribbled his name and number and handed it back. "Thanks, happy Fourth of July."

"Same to you and Bayou."

Ox nodded and turned to find Kate, without the surprise he was hoping to present.

"If it were meant to be, it would've been," he said softly to no one.

Weaving his way around the crowd to find his wife proved more challenging in the dark.

As the fireworks started, it lit the faces of those looking up at the colorful display in the sky. Ox used the flickering illumination and finally spotted her.

"Ox!" Kate cheered when he stepped next to her. "I was worried you wouldn't find us in time."

Kate wrapped her arm around him and pushed her side against his as the fireworks popped in the air.

"I'll always find you, my love." Ox rested his head on top of Kate's.

They watched as gold, pinks, and blue exploded in the sky above them.

Every day when Ox rose from the bed, he was grateful for another day with Kate and Bayou. But he wanted each day to be the best for his wife too. And letting the puppy slip through the cracks added to the regret already brewing heavy in his heart.

As the final fireworks filled the smoky sky, Ox took hold of Kate's chin and turned her face to his. He wrapped his arm tighter around her, pulling her into his chest. Pushing through the stiffness and fatigue, Ox kissed her and worried this would be the last Fourth of July he'd have as her husband.

Chapter 13

"They're still chatting," Kate whispered as Ox walked past in basketball shorts and his faded black T-shirt with a hole on the side.

"Don't eavesdrop," Ox warned. "Besides, you know Ali will tell you everything in the morning."

"I don't want to wait until the morning." Kate continued to peek through the cracked open door.

Bayou wedged his head between the door and the frame, forcing it open, sending Kate backward. Her feet scrambled to gain balance as the dog's paws scampered down the hall and were soon silenced by the living room's rug.

Kate hurried after him. When she reached the room, Ali and Matt were sitting on the couch with their backs to her. Bayou's big blocky head visibly stared at the bowl of popcorn nestled on the sofa between them.

"I'm so sorry," Kate muttered, walking around the couch in her mismatched pajama set. "Bayou, stop begging."

"He looks hungry." Ali tossed a kernel of popcorn at Bayou, who opened his mouth in time for it to land on his tongue.

Bayou smacked his lips like an elderly man without his dentures in and finished it with an upturn of his mouth.

"He has a resting hungry face." Kate put her hands on her hips.

Bayou sat back into his sloppy-sit and continued to eye Matt and Ali each time their hand went into the bowl. A bubble of drool formed in the corner of the dog's mouth.

Kate wrapped her hand around Bayou's collar. "Come on, let's go."

"Popcorn is dog kryptonite." Matt tossed some into his mouth as though to tease the dog.

Bayou remained seated as Kate gently pulled. "Bayou, leave it."

His vision focused straight ahead. And then, with a grunt, Bayou laid down, pulling Kate's hand, wrapped up in the collar, with him.

Her knees crashed to the rug, and she broke her fall with her left hand. "Bayou!"

The dog gave her a stern side glance. Matt and Ali laughed as Kate let go of Bayou's collar and sat back on her heels.

"Don't forget to turn off your nightlight." Kate pointed at Matt's nose.

He gasped.

"Your zit is barely noticeable in this light." Ali turned to Matt.

"That's an unfair jab, Kate. It's not my fault your dog is hilarious." Matt tossed a piece of popcorn at Bayou and then a few into his own mouth. "Ali was telling me about her favorite movies and food. Would you believe we like so many of the same things?"

"You don't say," Kate mentioned, standing up. "Can I get you both some wine?"

"Cabernet," they said in unison.

Ali sprung up. "Let me help you."

The women made their way into the kitchen while Bayou stayed with Matt and the popcorn.

Kate opened the small, under-the-counter wine refrigerator and removed a bottle of cabernet as Ali grabbed Kate's arm.

"He's so handsome. He belongs on the cover of a romance novel," Ali whispered and pushed her palm to her chest.

"Bayou or Matt?" Kate uncorked the bottle with a pop.

"Funny. Now, remind me why you didn't like him when you two were here that January."

"First, I was already falling for Ox. And second, he's not my type of guy. Remember, I told you he hit on me." Kate removed two glasses from the cupboard and then grabbed another one for herself.

"Right, how could I forget?" Ali bit her lower lip and peered around the kitchen's wall. "He seems younger than me."

"Not by much. Besides, you've always liked slightly younger guys."

Ali leaned onto her best friend. "They have more fun; they're not thinking about kids or buying some house with a white picket fence. I mean, who has time to maintain a white fence?"

"That's harsh. Families are a blessing, and not everyone who wants kids can have them, and those who can have them don't always want them. Go figure." Kate poured wine equally into the three glasses and handed Ali two of them.

"Kate." Ali pouted. "I'm sorry, I wasn't thinking."

Kate waved her off with the flick of her hand and took a long sip of the bold liquid. "It's fine. Ox and I knew before we were married that kids were not going to be in the cards."

Kate lowered the glass to the counter. "I just . . . I just wish everyone would stop asking us when we're going to have kids. It's never been an option, and I knew that when we married. But it doesn't seem to matter how many times we tell people we're not having kids; they still expect our story to change. And they never understand how it makes us feel to keep reminding them it's not happening. My parents don't come out and say it, but I know they think about it. And I worry Ox will take it personally. Maybe he already has. He's been acting off lately."

"He has?"

"Yes." Kate swigged a mouthful of wine.

"If it makes you feel better, it's statistically normal to have children, and not the other way around, so people don't mean to be rude about it." Ali put the wine glass to her nose, breathed in, and then took a sip.

"Yes, the fact that it's normal for people to have children makes me feel better that they won't stop asking." Kate had no choice but to roll her eyes as she tossed back another long gulp of wine.

"I'm not sure why I'm making this worse." Ali's hand reached out for Kate's arm. "I thought Ox and you were okay not having kids and getting more dogs?"

"I thought the same thing, but then when I brought up Bayou getting a sibling, he didn't even want to discuss it. And then tonight when I saw the puppy. Well," Kate ran her finger around the edge of the wine glass, "I guess he's having second thoughts."

"Maybe sit down and talk to him after this week's done. He seemed caught off guard with regards to the puppy tonight. You both have a lot going on, plus he lost one of his biggest joys. And to top it off, you're entertaining us and hosting Maggie's wedding."

Kate crossed her arms. "How could I've been so insensitive?"

"If it makes you feel better," Ali leaned in, "I think I'm crushing on Matt, and he'll be gone at the end of the week. So we can sulk together. Does that help?"

"Not really."

Before Kate could take another sip of wine, a knock at the front door echoed down the entryway. Bayou's soft bark was followed by the pattering of paws hurrying to the door.

"It's awful late for a visitor." Kate walked to the door, wineglass in hand, unsure who might be on the other side of the knock.

Slowly opening the door, a figure appeared under the patio light.

"Maggie?" Kate asked.

She stepped into the inn, tears streaming down her cheeks. "I can't do it. I can't marry Richard."

Chapter 14

Hearing the commotion outside of the bedroom, Ox climbed from the bed. His cane wasn't nearby, but he couldn't remember where he left it and used the walls for support.

When Ox entered the kitchen, his eyes squinted from the change in light. "Maggie?"

She was at the dining room table with Kate. Ali stood by the island holding a glass of wine. Bayou sat next to Maggie as she petted him, one of his paws rested on her leg. And Matt entered with a nearly empty bowl of popcorn clutched in his grip.

"I'm so sorry to bother you late like this," Maggie stated, her voice shaky.

Ox grabbed hold of the back of her chair and put his hand on her shoulder. "What happened?"

"Ali, do you want to join me back in the living room?" Matt asked.

Ali snatched up the bottle of wine on the island and carried it towards Matt.

Once Ali and Matt were in the living room, Ox sat down with Maggie, opposite his wife.

"I don't know what happened. Richard and I were admiring the night and a few fireworks we could see in the distance. Then, suddenly, every memory of Stan and I lit up in my heart. It was as though Stan was controlling those fireworks and exploding with anger over my engagement to Richard. My dear sweet Stan. And here I am about to marry another man? I can't do that to Stan. I'm not supposed to be with anyone else."

Maggie's tears fell, and Ox didn't know what to say. He looked at Kate, who kept rubbing her hand over the top of Maggie's hand.

He thought, closing his eyes as though the right words were hiding in the darkness.

"Maggie . . . " Ox patted her shoulder. "You love Richard, and Stan wouldn't want you to be alone. He'd want you to love and be loved."

"Everything with Richard happened so fast. I didn't plan or expect it." Maggie wiped her tears. "Gosh, I feel like such a fool."

"Don't say that." Kate leaned closer to Maggie and wrapped her arm around her.

"How embarrassing to be falling apart, but I didn't know where else to go."

"You don't have to be strong all the time," Ox stated.

"I needed to find peace and calm, and your inn was all I could think about." Maggie brushed a tear from her cheek.

"You know," Kate mentioned, "I have a great idea. A friend of mine has a boat," she waved her hand, "maybe it's a yacht. Anyways, we were going to go out tomorrow with Ali and Matt. How about instead, we make it an emergency girls-only day trip. It's the perfect time of year to be out on the water. The high for tomorrow is going to be in the low eighties. It'll be perfect." Kate smiled. "Ox, is it alright if you and Matt find something else to entertain yourselves with?"

He nodded. "Of course. I can catch up on a few things around here. And Matt and I can figure out something."

Kate looked at him and then back at Maggie. "Do you want to stay here tonight? We can leave right after breakfast."

"No." Maggie spread her hands out, and Ox caught her looking at her engagement band. "I can't impose."

"Don't worry. You're always welcome. Besides, Bayou would like it." Ox winked.

"Thank you, both." Maggie reached her hand out to Ox, and he gently held it.

He always thought of Maggie as a motherly figure and only wanted to see her happy. While Ox knew Richard and Maggie were a great couple, she needed time to process her feelings of apprehension. She'd helped him realize he needed to overcome his pride to keep Kate in his life, and now he hoped that his wife could do the same for Maggie tomorrow.

Chapter 15

The late morning sunlight reflected off the water and the shiny lacquered decks of the boats as Kate pulled into the parking spot.

A slight scent of salt and fish tickled her nose as all three women climbed from the 4Runner. However, Maggie's sun hat barely cleared the side door as she exited, causing her to appear as though she was in a fistfight to keep it on.

The marina was only twenty miles west of Crooked River and was undoubtedly the perfect location to film a movie based on a Debbie Macomber novel.

At the parking lot entrance to the marina was a compass laid out in bricks, and in the center, a wooden post ran at least ten feet high. A hanging basket of sherbet orange begonias was below a set of arrows facing different directions with locations carved into them.

Ali carted the insulated bag containing their drinks while Maggie carried a paper bag of snacks.

Kate unloaded Bayou from the back seat, and they traveled straight to a short bridge. The three of them and the dog crossed over it, bringing them to the horizontal dock that stretched wide in both directions. Reese's boat was a forty-foot yacht and had a slip off to the right.

"There it is." Kate pointed.

As they approached the yacht, Maggie's jaw hung open. "Wow."

"Right?" Kate grinned.

"Now that's luxury." Maggie continued to stare at the yacht.

"Reese lives on it during the summer months." Kate glanced around, but Reese was nowhere in sight.

Reese Huber, Kate's friend, and book club member, grew up on and around the Washington ports. Her father worked as a fisherman out of Seattle during her childhood and only recently retired. She spent nearly every weekend and school vacation with him, learning about the coves within the sound and the marine life that inhabited it. She was the perfect tour guide for today.

"*Her Yacht*?" Ali lifted her sunglasses up and onto her hairline, pointing at the back end of the yacht where the cobalt blue lettering appeared.

"It's a great name," a voice came, "don't want to confuse the men around here thinking that some man owns this beauty."

Reese, dressed in a white linen button-down shirt and jeans, popped her head up from the cabin. Her sun-kissed brown hair hung just below her ears in beachy waves. "Hi, Kate, it's been months — far too long."

"Captain Reese, permission to come aboard?" Kate saluted.

"Only if you brought snacks." Reese gestured a wave for the women to come on deck.

Kate stepped aside and allowed Maggie and then Ali to go first. Then she handed the leash off to Maggie, who directed Bayou onto the yacht with a worried half-leap from the perfectly level dock to boat ratio.

Kate grabbed hold of the rope and climbed over, giving Reese a long-awaited hug.

"We missed you at the last two book club meetings," Kate said. "Oh, where are my manners? Please meet Maggie and Ali. Of course, you know Bayou."

Reese turned and shook hands with the women. "Nice to meet you both."

Then Reese crouched down and took Bayou's face in her hands. "Who's my most favorite dog in the whole world?" She pressed her forehead against Bayou's forehead. "You are."

"Alright," Reese stood up and clapped her hands once, "I heard this is an emergency girls' party. And we're going to have fun."

Kate had carefully approached the whole Maggie's cold-feet-being-un-sure-about-marrying-Richard thing to Reese, and she said she would come up with the perfect plan to help Maggie overcome any doubts.

The yacht left the port and gently made its way out into the bay as Kate strapped on Bayou's life vest. She loved the English Lab but couldn't deny the fact that if they needed to swim for it, he'd sink like an anchor after a minute of dog paddling.

The water shimmered in deep shades of shadowy blues as the yacht cut through the surface like scissors to a ribbon. Steep rocky cliffs with evergreens growing at their edges framed the peninsula as they came to a clearing.

Bayou rested on the floor; the reflectors on his life vest nearly blinded Kate when the sun's rays beamed off them.

"I thought we'd head over to Ebey's Island." Reese pulled a gray baseball hat over her hair. "There's a dock. It's in pretty rough shape, but we can tie it off there. The little island is perfect for exploring, especially in the summer. And because it's a bit tricky to get over there, we probably won't see another soul."

"That sounds lovely." Maggie wrapped her hands around her knee and leaned back into the seat.

This morning, over Earl Grey tea, coffee, and French toast, Maggie only talked about the weather. Ali and Matt had sat with less than a breath between them, stealing smiles from each other between bites.

"Ali, tell me about what happened last night?" Kate asked.

"I'm not sure what you're referring to?" Ali smirked and lowered her sunglasses on her nose.

Kate gave her best friend a look of annoyance. "You know exactly what I mean."

Ali stretched her neck out at the view. Today she wore khaki shorts, a white tank top, and a yellow button-up tied at the side of her stomach. Kate removed her camera from the bag and snapped some photos.

"I'm going to send this to *Yachts Are Us Magazine*." Kate set her camera in her lap. "Now spill."

Ali pushed her sunglasses back up on her nose. "Fine."

Kate smiled, and Maggie turned to Ali.

"We stayed up until maybe one or two in the morning. And about midnight, we realized we might be keeping everyone awake. So, we headed into the backyard and sat around the fire pit. It was a nice temperature outside, and snuggling under a blanket made it perfect. Sorry, we finished off that bottle of wine and might've polished off a box of crackers." Ali laughed.

"What did you talk about?" Kate asked.

"Everything and nothing. It was one of those conversations where you discuss your childhood memories and your adult dreams. Matt and I have so much in common it's almost weird how compatible we seem."

"Sounds promising." Kate winked.

"We're having a good time getting to know each other. And at the end of the week, we'll say our goodbyes and promise to keep in touch. However, we know as the months fade, so will our long-distance communication." Ali's hair danced in the breeze. "It'll be like after summer camp."

"I miss summer camp. Nothing like having a vacation from your parents' rules." Kate pushed her windblown curls out of her face. "What about you, Maggie? Do you think opposites make the best couples or are similarities the best?"

Maggie unlaced her hands from around her knee. "I don't think there's a right or a wrong way to go about what works best. It's an individual preference. Stan and I were opposites in many ways but also had many complementing elements."

"And what about you and Richard?" Kate encouraged.

"Richard and I are more alike than we are opposite, and I believe that allows us to showcase other qualities in our relationship. Even if you have many things in common, you still need to be an individual within yourself. Otherwise, you'll be stepping on each other's toes left and right."

"What are your thoughts, Reese?" Kate raised her voice over the sound of the water breaking against the hull.

Reese focused on the horizon as they continued out into the bay and further from the mainland. "I'm not the one to give relationship advice. I don't even have a pet."

The women shared a laugh.

Kate slid the cooler bag toward her by yanking on the zipper. "I'm thirsty. Anyone else?"

Ali took a peek at her cell phone. "Technically, it's two in the morning in Shanghai, so it's definitely time for a drink."

Maggie sat forward. "By that account, I do believe we're late to the party."

Bayou got to his feet and shook himself as though a shiver traveled through him from head to tail. Kate handed the women, except for Reese, a can of rosé wine.

"I never would've thought a dog would need a life vest." Ali cracked open her can.

"He can swim, but not far." Kate rubbed the top of the dog's head.

"Wine in a can?" Maggie inspected the container.

"This was rated one of the best in those wine magazines." Kate looked the label over. "It's nice some things never change, like long lines at the grocery store so you can flip through the magazines on the rack."

Maggie wasted no time and tapped the top of the can before popping it open. Ali scrolled her cell phone's screen with her thumb.

"Kate's right. It's listed as a top wine pick." Ali wedged the can between her legs. "But shouldn't we drink it from a cup or glass?"

"Live a little," Reese called back over her shoulder.

"I've lived a lot." Ali crossed her arm over her chest.

Kate knew Ali and Reese had similar personalities, which meant they were strong-willed and opinionated, but Kate hoped they wouldn't butt heads too much today. Not to mention Reese was doing a nice thing by taking them out for free. Typically, she charged a small fortune for an outing. With Bayou's therapy lessons mostly in limbo, she wasn't sure where they'd make the extra money they needed to help cover her and Ox's private medical insurance.

Without looking, Kate reached back into the bag and pulled out a can for herself. As she cracked it open, liquid shot up like a firework. A squeal came from Kate's mouth as her hand stretched out and away from her body.

"Oh goodness!" Ali leaned back from the geyser foaming over Kate's hand.

"I packed soda and wine." Kate shook her hand as the sticky liquid rolled off it. "I thought this was wine."

Bayou licked the sweet goodness from Kate's hand as she reached for a wet wipe from her backpack and wiped up what Bayou hadn't licked up. "We're here to listen to anything anyone might want to discuss. Any uncertainties in life or upcoming events."

"I can take a hint." Maggie sighed.

Kate sipped the soda; she'd have to wait on the wine. "Please share."

"I supposed I can't escape from it." Maggie gestured at the yacht in the middle of the open water. "I love Richard, but something's causing guilt to well up inside my heart—the guilt of remarrying. And then I think about Richard's late wife. It feels like I'm replacing her. I think of Stan. I do believe they're in Heaven, looking down, and it haunts my decision."

The yacht entered into a tiny cove and slowed its speed.

"Have you and Richard talked about this?" Kate inquired.

"No," Maggie said. "I did what I thought was best. I ran away like a child. It sounds funny when I say it aloud. Hey, honey, I believe our spouses are judging us from Heaven, so watch out for lightning bolts."

"If you believe in that, have you tried asking for a sign?" Reese asked over her shoulder.

"What do you mean?" Maggie wrapped her hands around her can.

"I'm a firm believer that whether you believe in God, the Universe, or something else, there are always signs." Reese pointed the yacht toward the shore. "Whether supernatural or in nature, it finds a way of showing you, opening your eyes. That's why I love being out on the water or hiking up a mountain. Getting away from life's clutter of being told this and that, versus discovering it for yourself."

Maggie studied her can. "I guess my faith and hope are lacking."

"Maybe we can help you strengthen your resolve today," Reese suggested.

Kate could see the doubt creasing Maggie's face as her hat flopped in the wind, but she hoped Reese was correct.

Chapter 16

Matt grimaced as he set his coffee mug on the table, his hand cupping it from the top. "Kate reminded me when I arrived, but I thought I could power through and drink regular coffee. I can't believe you still don't have an espresso machine."

"The good news is there's zero snow on the ground, so if you want to run into town and get your fancy nutter flutter, you can borrow my truck." Ox raised his cup of steaming black coffee. "Didn't your father ever tell you that strong coffee makes a strong man?"

"My father and I rarely speak about anything other than mathematics, technology, and career success." Matt crossed his arms. "And what do you think espresso is? It's the strongest coffee."

"Technically, the lighter the roast, the more caffeine there is in it. So unless you're referring to taste, espresso is weak." He took a long sip of the rich liquid.

Ox had woken up grateful for the day. When the sun rose, he turned over and watched Kate sleep. Of course, seeing his wife in the morning light always made everything better, even if it was a bad day filled with symptoms from his MS and thoughts of what was to come.

Since he and Kate had married and moved in together, they didn't spend a lot of time apart. Her photography gigs only caused her to be gone for a few hours here and there, and Kate was always home by dinner time. Plus, she could arrange her schedule anyway she liked, allowing her to help around the inn with the guests when he had to do a therapy flying lesson.

"I thought Bayou never left your side?" Matt asked.

"Usually, but I wanted him to be there for Maggie. Plus, I can't deny a dog a ride on the open water."

Ox set his coffee mug on the table and stood up. "I know I told the women yesterday we'd figure out something to do, but I don't want to hold you back if you have plans for today."

"I thought it'd be amazing to tackle High Rock Lookout. I've heard Mount Rainier is beautiful this time of year, and the view of it from there should be spectacular."

"That would be a great adventure, plus the snow should be cleared except for near the summit."

"You're coming, right?"

Ox scratched at his beard. "I can't do activities like that anymore."

"Sorry, man." Matt cringed.

"Don't apologize."

"What about adaptive bikes? I've seen people use them on some of the trails."

"Not enough hand or leg strength to make those items work for me on the mountains around here. But a good thought, Kate had it too."

Matt played with the stud in his ear. "I assumed we would be doing things as a group. And you did say your truck was available for a coffee run."

"We'll do some more group activities, but today's detour is trying to save Maggie from calling off the wedding. Your phone's GPS will help you get right where you need to go." Ox headed down the hall to the office. "Let me get you the keys."

As he snatched the truck keys out of the desk drawer, he paused. His entire office was a reminder of his past and the incredible opportunities he had before multiple sclerosis dug its horrible claws into his nervous system.

Ox met Matt as he was heading upstairs to his room. "Here you go." He tossed the keys straight up.

Matt caught them. "Thanks again."

Ox headed back to his office and shut the door. He couldn't recall the last time he sat in there completely alone.

He lowered himself into the desk chair and faced it toward the door. A photo above the light switch provided a stream of memories.

He inspected the picture from their first summer together. He and Kate were on the ferry to Whidbey Island on a rare cold July day. No one wanted to spend the day strolling around town or on the outside deck of the ferry boat with the chilly wind against their faces. And when he noticed they were alone, he took her camera and snapped the photo of her with the Puget Sound in the background. The way Kate stood, tilting her head, bravely facing the world without hesitation.

On his short bookcase opposite the desk was a collection of aviation books and manuals. Using his feet, he propelled the chair within reach of the low shelves.

Ox pulled a book to the edge one by one, watching them topple onto the floor with repetitive thunks. With each book removed, neuropathy inched through his fingertips.

Lowering onto the floor, Ox began ripping pages by gripping the paper between the palms of his hands. But the weakness made each tear harder than the last.

When he could no longer rip the pages, he chucked the books at the wall. They smacked against the wall and crashed to the floor. With his final throw, the book sailed into the framed photo of Kate on the ferry. Glass shattered, but the frame remained hanging on the wall.

The photo reminded him of his New Year's resolution: Stop allowing the past to take control of the present. He hated himself for being negative and for pushing back whenever someone invited him out for activities. Yet, all he could think about was the past and how much he was dragging Kate down with him.

Chapter 17

The yacht bobbed in the shore's high tide as Reese steered it to the side of a long weather-beaten dock. Rocks and driftwood met the slight crash of waves as a thin set of clouds stretched across the baby blue sky. A few short steps inland and the landscape jetted straight up like skyscrapers in downtown Seattle.

Reese moved the throttle lever and pressed some buttons on the dash of the driver's area. "I'm going to tie us off."

One by one, they stepped onto the dock, which swayed reluctantly under their shoes. Reese helped Kate with Bayou, ensuring that he cleared the relatively easy transition from the yacht to the deck.

"There's a small trail we can follow to the top." Reese pointed to the right, where a clearing between the wild grasses met a rough trail.

Kate shoved two quilts under her arms and instructed Bayou to go with Maggie. Ali carried the snacks, and Reese had the beverage bag.

"This area is beautiful. I can't wait to see the views." Maggie weaved through the slippery moss-covered rocks with Bayou on her heels.

The breeze picked up, sending a mist of moisture their way as Kate's unruly curls whipped around. She stopped, pulled a clip from her purse, and secured her hair.

The other women made their way up the embankment, with Bayou in front of Maggie but behind Reese.

Kate paused and took in the view, noticing how the tide appeared to be on its way out but didn't second guess Reese's nautical expertise.

When the women reached the top of the cliff, evergreens scattered the land around the edges. Beyond it was a thin carpet of grass and bold dark rocks the size of cars.

Above, the clouds started to gray and thicken, but the temperature remained warm as the sun peeked through.

"The rocks over there make for great tables." Reese pointed as they continued toward the middle of the landform.

Reaching the spot, Kate took one of the quilts and shook it out over the rock as though putting it on a bed. The blue and green patterned fabric squares blended with the landscape around them.

Ali unloaded the snacks and set them up buffet-style on a neighboring rock. Bayou picked a spot near Maggie and rested against the side of the rock.

"This looks great. I'm hungry." Kate grabbed a paper plate from Ali.

"It should. It's all from your kitchen," Ali stated.

Kate handed a plate to Maggie, who took it but didn't move from her spot.

"Want me to grab you some food?" Kate wiggled her paper plate.

"No, you girls go first. I'm taking in the view." Maggie half-smiled.

Kate stacked her plate with crackers, strawberries, two of the four kinds of cheeses, prosciutto, and mini chocolate chips.

Ali followed behind, taking a sampling of everything but the strawberries. After Reese handed out cans of rosé, she filled her plate with snacks and joined the rest of them on the rock.

Maggie's eyes studied the view, holding the empty plate to her chest while Bayou focused on each bite they took.

As the clouds continued to grow thicker, Kate reached into her backpack and removed a light sweater, resting it on her shoulders like a boyfriend's letterman jacket.

"Stan always loved the views in the Pacific Northwest. We often went to places like this and hiked around. Picnic lunches were the staple of our weekends." Maggie eased off the rock, collected a few nibbles of food, and returned.

"I wish Ox and I could go out and do more things like this. He can go from being his old, adventurous self to being unable to leave the inn with the flip of a switch." Kate covered her mouth. "Don't mention that to him, please." She rubbed her fingers together, removing the dampness left over from the fresh strawberries. "Sometimes, it just gets me down, and I can't help but complain. I want so much for him to find ways to still do what he loves."

"I agree. Ox does need to get out more when he can." Maggie nibbled the cracker. "Life's not perfect, and unless we complain once in a while, we might forget we're not alone in our frustrations. Richard's good about allowing me to complain. I never feel like I can't talk to him about things." The rest of the cracker remained between Maggie's fingers. "Except right now."

"You're not complaining about getting married." Kate folded a piece of prosciutto like a ribbon onto her slice of Gouda. "You're only watching out for your feelings."

"What type of sign do you think would help show you that marrying Richard is the right thing to do?" Reese tossed a mini square of Muenster cheese into her mouth.

"I'm not sure I know." Maggie picked at the strawberries on her plate.

"There's such a different visual perspective of the area up here." Ali sipped her rosé. "The way sunshine falls across some of the land and leaves other spots of dark shadows blanketed from clouds. We can see the sun is out, but over on the mainland, they can't because they're not able to see the whole picture from the ground."

Kate took in a deep breath as though trying to inhale the entire view. Like everything in life, a different perspective always made for a more precise insight.

"Life's full of clouds and sunshine. We all need to hold tight until it's our time to see the light," Reese added.

"Those clouds are building fast." Ali pointed. "I thought it was supposed to be sunny all day?"

"Convergence zone," Kate and Reese said in unison.

"We might end up with snow before the day is over," Ali added with a chortle.

"Now, that would be an interesting turn of events." Maggie munched on a piece of cheese and tossed one to Bayou, who caught it in his mouth. "Okay, girls, talk to me about something fun. Ali, what are your plans for the rest of the year?"

"You're as awesome at avoidance as Kate is." Ali took a swig of wine. "Let's say I'm juggling a few things, but hopefully not for long."

"Juggling sounds interesting." Reese adjusted her baseball hat.

"Not by choice." Ali leaned back on the rock and gazed up at the sky. "I worked in Shanghai for over a year. And as hard as it is to admit, I've lost my compass. But I'll find my way again."

"What's your biggest fear?" Maggie asked.

Ali propped her feet up on the rock. "I don't have any."

Maggie laughed. "We all have fears, big and small."

"Ali has a fear of settling down," Kate blurted.

"It's not a fear." Ali sat up, crossed her legs, and readjusted the plate on her lap. "It's a lifestyle choice."

The wind traveled through the evergreens and caused Maggie's sun hat to flutter.

"And what's your lifestyle choice?" Reese asked.

Ali shifted on the rock. "Adventure, planning, and self-reliance."

"Do you enjoy being single and traveling?" Maggie tossed another wedge of Gouda into Bayou's mouth.

"I do love those things, but sometimes I sit alone at night and wonder what sharing moments with someone else would be like," Ali stated.

As Ali's best friend, it was her job to know and understand her. The only way she could ever be the best-best friend was to find a way to help Ali.

"Kate, don't pout. I choose never to bring it up." Ali folded her hands around her knees.

"But we talk about everything." Kate held tight to her plate as the wind attempted to tip it up off her lap. "I thought."

"Like mentioning being frustrated about your and Ox's lack of adventures?" Ali retorted. "Or the other thing?"

Yeah, the baby thing.

"Matt's cute, right?" Kate shoved a mozzarella ball in her mouth like a hungry chipmunk.

"That was an abrupt change of subject." Ali's cheeks turned rosy as she threw a chocolate chip at Kate's head. "He's cute, and he smells like a manly ocean."

Kate rubbed at the side of her temple where the chocolate had bounced off. "What's a manly ocean?"

They started laughing, and as it grew louder, it drew out longer. Kate wrapped her arm around her stomach. As tears pricked the edges of her eyes, she gasped for air, finally able to inhale a few breaths.

The laughter separated and slowed between them.

"As soon as we finish up, let's go for a walk around the top of the cliff. If the clouds are clear on the other side, we might be able to make out Mt. Rainier." Reese stuck the last piece of food into her mouth.

"I would like to get some photos of us before the day is over." Kate lifted the camera she'd removed from her backpack.

They continued to watch the clouds form as the sun engaged in a game of peek-a-boo. When their plates were clean, they placed their garbage into a grocery bag, and Kate tied it at the handles.

"Leave the stuff here. We'll grab it on our way down," Reese instructed as she finished her wine and switched to a can of soda.

Together they made their way through the tall grass and yellow wildflowers. Kate missed scouting out the landscape with others. Her camera had been the one constant on her adventures, but being with friends made the trips more meaningful.

Bayou trotted ahead at first but soon fell behind as he sniffed his way along. And then something small with a fluffy tan tail jetted up a tree trunk. The dog's head jerked upward and at the tree. Kate did her best to watch her step and keep an eye on Bayou.

"Bayou, leave it."

His nose twitched, and his ears pinned to the sides of his head.

"Leave it," Kate warned again as she drew closer to him.

The terrain might've been solid, but it was as lumpy as the top of a walnut brownie.

With Kate's next step, the front of her shoe hit something substantial, like a root from a tree, and she jetted forward, landing with a thump.

"We have a Kate down! A Kate is down!" Ali ran back to her as Kate popped her head up and pushed her stomach off the hard-packed ground.

Bayou hovered over her, licking the back of her neck.

"We have a Kate down a lot." Maggie stood in a wide stance a few feet further up the trail. "I don't know how you manage to be so clumsy."

"Bayou, I'm okay. Your licks are not helping." Kate shooed the dog away.

Ali reached her hand out, hoisted Kate up, and helped brush the grass from her knees. "I'm pretty sure the real reason why you and Ox don't go out on adventures has nothing to do with his MS."

Kate couldn't help but laugh because it might be true.

Bayou forged ahead with Maggie and Reese while Ali and Kate brought up the rear, easing her sore knees back into action.

The breeze cooled her cheeks as it blew past. Then Kate paused, took the camera lens cap off, and snapped a few quick shots of the women with the view of the water around them nearing the edge of the cliff. She had an upcoming collection for a set of greeting cards with an August due date, and she only needed a few more images.

Reese pointed. "I can see Mt. Rainier."

Ali stopped and followed Reese's finger. "Oh, yes. I wonder who's hiking up it today."

"Maybe a person's soul mate." Reese adjusted her hat.

"Probably several peoples' soul mates." Kate watched as she stepped over a log that had fallen across the path.

The women stopped and turned, appearing in a line like The Rockettes — Summer Edition — with less glittery outfits and hiking boots instead of high heels.

"Thank you, girls. I appreciate the time you're spending with me today." Maggie made eye contact with each of them, and her face brightened.

The clouds overhead grew darker as the wind kicked up again.

"Stupid Washington weather." Kate shivered.

Reese's eyes went to the sky. "We should probably head back. I don't want to be out if the weather turns bad."

They made their way to the rocks and gathered up their belongings as the sky darkened to a smoke-gray and the wind shook the trees' branches. As they approached the edge of the path to descend back down, Kate spotted it first.

"Reese, what happened?" Kate pointed at the apparent low tide as the water level made the dock appear taller than when they arrived.

The pylons were more noticeable, and the sand exposed many feet out from the shore. The yacht's underside was now visible from where they stood.

"We appear to be grounded." Reese's shoulders dropped.

Chapter 18

Waking from his nap on the couch, Ox noticed the inn sat as still as a forest after a snowfall. Rarely was he without Bayou, and the sense of loneliness had begun to fill his heart.

He moved to the edge of the couch and got his bearings. Then, with his cane in his right hand, he pushed himself to stand.

At the entertainment center, he searched for some music to play when the phone rang in the office.

Rushing as quickly as he could out of the living room, he reached the office where the stark reminder of what occurred a few hours ago greeted him.

Carefully stepping around the broken glass and torn apart books, he answered the phone. "Hello, Inn of the Woods."

"Ox, this is Doctor Ebbinga. I work over at the Crooked River Hospital's Oncology Department and received your information from Victoria."

Ox pulled out the desk chair and sank into it. "How might I help you?"

"Actually, I'm calling about Bayou, but since he's a dog, I figured I needed to talk to you." The doctor chuckled. "A little dog humor. Any-who, I've been informed Bayou will be helping out Victoria's sister and my patient, Leslie. I wanted to reach out and see if you and Bayou would be up to taking on a few other patients of mine."

Ox shifted in the chair. "I . . . "

"I'm aware people don't like being in a hospital, it's not Disneyland, but that feeling can be diminished with the help of a dog like Bayou. I have three other patients who I think would benefit greatly."

"It's just that . . . " Ox took a deep breath.

"It was not only Victoria who raved about your dog. My long-time friends, the MacArthurs, mentioned Bayou had helped them out with their fear of flying."

"Bayou enjoyed working with them; they always had extra treats for him." Ox stared at the picture of Bayou in front of his plane parked in the hangar. "If I could take some time to think about it and get back to you?"

"Sure, when you decide, please give me a call. Oh, I should mention, as with Leslie, the insurance company will pay you since I'm prescribing it. Now, if I could only prescribe chocolate cake." Again, the doctor chuckled.

Ox huffed a laugh. "Thank you, Doctor Ebbinga. I'll be in touch."

When Ox hung up, he dropped his head into his hands, he closed his eyes. At least the doctor had a sense of humor which probably helped his patients more than he realized.

Ox rested his elbows on the top of his knees and clasped his hands together. "How could I have been blind to the lack of financial help Bayou's therapy would cause?"

Sure the inn and Kate's photography brought in enough money to live off, but carrying private medical insurance was far from cheap. Even without upkeep on the Cessna's maintenance and fuel, they needed the extra cash from Bayou's therapy services.

"I have no choice but to take on more than just Leslie." He pushed his hands through the sides of his hair.

Ox peered out his office window at the assortment of green treetops. Summer was such a beautiful time of year.

"Now, I regret not getting a boating license and using Bayou's therapy for people afraid of the open water."

Taking his thumb, he pushed his wedding ring back and forth on his finger. Admittedly, Ox often thought about continuing to support Kate and himself for years to come. It wasn't that she couldn't support herself; it came down to his medical care and handling the inn full time. If he continued to deteriorate, he'd have no choice but to hire outside help or stop running the inn. Money was the root of all evil — but money could also be a saving grace.

He checked the time on the desk clock, four thirty-eight. Kate, Ali, and Maggie must be having a blast, but he expected them to be back by dinner time. However, Matt would most certainly be late. The hike, plus the drive, could keep him out until at least dark.

Removing the trash basket from under his desk, he used the chair again to scoot around the office. Each aviation book and manual went into the basket as though saying goodbye to a good friend. A great friend. A best friend.

Ox used his cane to stand, and his stomach moaned. "Dinner. And tomorrow, the wedding."

If it was still on.

"Of course, it's still on," he said, grabbing the dustbuster from the hall closet. "They love each other."

With the glass cleaned up, the office didn't look any different than this morning, minus the now empty bookshelf. He removed the broken frame from the wall and laid it down on the desk.

His nap had helped some, so Ox headed to the kitchen to put his talents to work and pulled out the ingredients for the perfect summer dinner.

He placed the raw salmon into a glass pan and whisked teriyaki sauce, soy sauce, and some fresh lemon with a fork in a small bowl. After pouring the mixture over the fish, he set it in the refrigerator and put a timer on the stove to remind him to flip the salmon and let it marinate on the other side.

Even with Bayou gone, there was enough fur on the floors to construct Bayou 2.0, so Ox got busy sweeping and mopping.

Afterward, he stripped the bedding from the master bedroom bed and tossed it in the washing machine. Ox always found solace in keeping busy with chores as he cranked the sound up on the CD player blasting Pearl Jam's *Vitalogy* album.

It wasn't until the timer dinged that Ox realized how late it had gotten. He should've at least heard something from Kate by now. But she was with others, and he knew a little wine and beautiful summer weather often caused Washingtonians to forget about the time.

"At least it's still light for a few more hours." Ox shut off the music and turned on the television, selecting *The Fugitive* off the movie shelf.

He would've preferred to read, but he didn't have a current book, and he wasn't going to dive into the rom-com novel Kate had left lying around.

As the movie started, Ox looked at his cell phone every five minutes and did everything he could to keep from listening for a vehicle coming up the driveway.

Chapter 19

"What do you mean, grounded?" Kate challenged.

"Similar to run-a-ground, only technically since the yacht was not moving at the time, it's called grounded." Reese headed down the cliff's trail. "We'll have to wait for high tide to come back in, and then we can leave."

"But how'd this happen?" Kate asked.

"We don't even need the dock to get onto the yacht." Ali pointed.

"Mistakes happen to the best of us." Maggie pushed her hand into the top of her hat as the wind tried to steal it.

Reese turned to glance at Kate and continued making her way down the path. "It's a soft grounding, so there's no damage to the hull. We just need to wait for the tide to come back in."

"Hold on a minute," Kate whispered, catching up. "Something isn't adding up. You know the tide tables."

Ali and Maggie had separated from the group, but Bayou remained some thirty feet up the path between them.

Reese smiled. "I figured a little scare might be what Maggie needs to help her get over her uncertainty about the wedding."

Kate pressed her lips together. "That's a bit risky."

"Yes, and no," Reese said, her voice still low. "I'm experienced on the water; I didn't do anything we can't easily get out of in a few hours. But this storm was not something I planned for." She eyed the sky.

"Does that mean we should be worried? Because it seems like we should be worried." Kate's heart rate went from normal to rapid in a split second.

"No, don't worry. Besides, what's the worst that can happen?" Reese shrugged her shoulders.

"*A Perfect Storm, Adrift, All is Lost.* I can go on. My movie trivia skills are outstanding." With each stomp on the downward grade of the path, Kate's body vibrated up through her boots.

"It's fine and a great reminder of why you should always bring enough wine and snacks."

"What about Ox and Matt? They'll be expecting us back for dinner." The tip of Kate's boot hit a rock, and she stumbled. Her right hand jetted out as Reese grabbed hold of it.

"I can see why Ox worries about you." She laughed. "Goodness."

Once she regained her balance, Kate removed her cell phone from her back pocket. "I should at least call Ox and let him know we'll be late."

"Good luck, there's no service out here."

"This isn't Alaska." Kate held her phone out in front of her checking the signal strength in the corner. "I can see land and a city across the sound." She pointed.

"What's going on?" Ali said, her voice sharp like a boss in a conference meeting.

"Looks like we're going to be stuck here for a while." Kate paused on the trail, waiting for Ali and Maggie.

Bayou caught up, and she petted his head. His jowls flapped in the gusts of wind. Darkness coated the bottom of the sky; the last of the pale blue had disappeared.

"I hope you ladies packed a poncho, or we can all squeeze below deck," Maggie warned. "It won't be long before it starts to rain. My knees have alerted me."

Ali and Kate continued down the path until they gathered at the bottom with Bayou.

"Kate, did you call Ox and let him know we'll be late?" Maggie removed her five-year-old cell phone from her light sweater's pocket.

"No signal, sorry, Maggie." Kate frowned.

Anxiety spread across Maggie's face, starting with her eyes as they searched around. Kate watched as Maggie swallowed uncomfortably and her mouth parted.

"I see." Maggie passed them with a blank stare and headed in the direction of Reese and the dock.

Ali turned to Kate and crossed her arms over her chest. The temperature had dropped with the disappearance of the sun, and there was now a crisp chill in the wind. Waves crashed against the exposed rocks from the low tide and downed timbers bobbing in the wake.

"Is this the time I should mention that I didn't bring a jacket?" Ali's eyes grew wide.

"Why not?" Kate blinked.

"I didn't pack one that went with this outfit. It's in storage. It's summertime. When does Washington ever get a summer storm?" Ali looked up.

"There have been a few, rare, but still." Kate bit her lip and tapped her boot on the dock's planks as they creaked and moaned. "All I have is this thin sweater."

Ali grimaced like she'd smelled the exhaust of an old truck.

They locked arms, and with Bayou at Kate's side, they met back up with Reese and Maggie at the front of the yacht.

"Look on the bright side," Reese declared, "we have more time to snack."

"Is it safe to get on board?" Ali stretched her neck as she attempted to peer around it.

"Yes, completely safe the keel is stuck in the sand. It's more stable than when the water level is where it should be at." Reese held out her hand for Ali.

Ali took it and climbed up, followed by Maggie. Kate was last with Bayou. The yacht was an even worse jump for him than when they arrived. She patted the vessel where he needed to put his paws. Then grabbing his backside, Kate raised him as his front paws found the edge of the yacht's gunnel. As she pushed him up further, his paws started to slide, and Kate panicked. With all the strength she had, Kate heaved Bayou forward. He cleared the side and had all four paws on the yacht as she descended backward, her arms swimming in the air. Her bottom thumped on the dock. She turned her head in time for the camera that'd hung around her neck to hit her chest.

When she opened her eyes and turned her head back to center, the women's faces leaned over the yacht along with Bayou's head.

Kate rubbed her sternum as she pushed herself to a sitting position. The wetness of the deck and leftover sandy footprints seeped through her jeans to her underwear.

"Are you okay?" they asked in unison.

Kate rolled over, crawled to a downward dog, and stood. She grabbed her bag and brushed off as much wet sand as she could.

Once Kate was on the yacht, she rested her hand between her ribcage. "That's going to be a pretty bruise."

Bayou weaved between her legs as she moved further to the middle of the deck. The dampness of Kate's clothing caused shivers to travel through her body.

Reese appeared with a stack of blankets. "Kate, I've set out a change of clothes for you in the head."

"Thanks." Kate made her way past the women and down the few steps, taking her below deck.

Bayou followed as far as he could and then laid at the steps' landing with a heavy sigh. Pistol Annies played from the speakers as Kate shut the bathroom door.

When Kate climbed the steps to return to the deck, she laughed at herself in the new outfit.

"Sorry, it's been a while since I went through my clothes down there and didn't realize I only had pajamas." Reese clenched her teeth and smiled wide like an emoji.

"I'm going to guess it was around December?" Kate pulled at the long sleeve pajama shirt with reindeer and decorated balsam trees.

"I'm right on point with Christmas in July," Reese said.

Kate flopped down next to Ali, focusing on Maggie, who stared off at the landscape in the distance. The scent of salty air rose off the water.

Reese handed each of them a blanket and joined them on the bench as Bayou leaned against the side of Kate's leg. The wind whistled past her ears, and thunder rumbled like trash cans quickly dragged to the curb on collection day. The open back of the yacht wouldn't give them the protection they'd need from a coming storm; soon, they'd have to huddle below deck.

When Maggie faced Kate, tears were forming at the rims of her eyes. "I've been a fool." Taking the blanket, she wrapped it tighter around her shoulders; her hands disappeared behind the fabric she clutched.

"Don't say that." Kate rested her hand on top of Bayou's head.

"When I saw that we might be stranded, I panicked. I instantly thought of Richard and how much I wanted to hug him and see his face, hear his voice." Maggie looked down at the table and backed up again, wiping a tear. "How lucky to be able to love again and be loved. Stan would want me to be happy."

A bolt of lightning tore through the sky. The crack of thunder followed almost immediately as drops of rain plopped on the table's top. The women turned their heads toward the heavens.

"Does this thing not have a cover?" Ali looked around.

"Yes, but the canopy is torn, and I haven't ordered a new one yet." Reese pressed her finger against her chin. "We never have summer storms."

"A sign," Maggie whispered. "Stan always loved storms. He used to say storms were nature's way of revitalizing a sleepy Earth."

Kate tilted her head and smiled. Through the speakers under the low rumbling, Maren Morris, "I Could Use a Love Song" played.

"I think this just turned into a bachelorette party yacht!" Reese threw her hands up in the air. She danced to the driver's area and messed with a button causing the volume to rise, vibrating the speakers.

"I'll get us some wine," Kate declared.

"I think we're going to need some chocolate. I have some leftover goodies for just this occasion." Reese hurried down the steps to the galley.

Maggie tossed her hat on the table but kept the blanket and stood. She instantly swayed her hips to the beat of the music. Kate waved Ali to come and join them.

Ali crossed her arms. "It's raining."

"It's my party, and I say join us." Maggie's shoulders wiggled, and her arms swung from side to side.

"Yes, if Maggie can do the hula in the middle of a rainstorm, you can at least stand next to us." With her sunglasses still on, Kate closed her eyes and tilted her head to the sky.

The raindrops splashed on her cat-eye sunglasses, and when she moved her head back down, she couldn't see out of them.

"Your sunglasses look like a rear window without a wiper blade." Ali's voice was next to her.

Kate turned, using both her pointer fingers, and pressed them on her sunglasses. As she rubbed them back and forth like blades, she stuck her tongue out at her best friend.

Ali whooped a laugh, and Kate grabbed her hands, swinging them back and forth as "Whose Bed Have Your Boots Been Under" came on.

With each new song, the tide rose, and once Kate stood still, she noticed the yacht beginning to sway.

"I think we should be good to head back now." Reese turned down the music.

Maggie ran her hand through her wet hair and then rubbed her arms with her hands. "Do you mind if we go sit below and warm up?"

"Be my guest. There are towels down there, and you'll find the snacks on the table." Reese started up the engine.

As it vibrated to life, foamy bubbles rose around the stern.

Everyone except Reese headed down the steps as Bayou laid at the edge, his watchful eyes on them. They crowded around the small table with a bowl of powdered sugar-coated chocolate and peanut butter squares, chocolate-covered almonds, and pretzel sticks.

Kate felt the yacht's rearward momentum pushing its way through the water, and she hoped Ox was not too worried about her and Bayou.

She checked the time on her cell phone, not realizing it was past the regular time they served dinner at the inn. Typing out a text, she crossed her fingers that it went through sooner rather than later.

Chapter 20

From the back patio, Ox watched the storm moving in from the southwest. Thankfully he hadn't set up for tomorrow, as the rain would have quickly soaked everything.

The creak of the front door opening echoed to the back patio and reminded Ox that he still needed to oil it. He hurried inside and shut the French doors behind him.

Matt appeared and dropped his backpack on the entry rug.

"Wow, Ox, you were right. Amazing views on the mountain today." Matt glanced around. "Why is it so dark in here?"

Ox punched the TV's remote off, darkening the screen. He then made his way to the bank of light switches for the living room and flipped them on. A warm glow filled the room, and the storm outside no longer felt like it was coming through the windows.

"Is Ali here?" Matt peered around.

"None of them are back yet." Ox ran his hand through his hair. "I haven't heard from Kate, no text or calls."

Matt removed his cell phone from his front pocket. "When were they supposed to be back?"

Ox shrugged. "I would've thought by now."

"Have you called?" Matt picked up his backpack and made his way to the stairs.

"I called, but no answer. Do you have Ali's number?"

Matt shook his head. "No, but have you checked her social media? Maybe she posted."

"I don't have any of those things."

Matt turned, lowered to the first step, and untied his boots with one hand. Multitasking, he used his free hand to scroll through his phone. "I don't see any new posts. Let me go clean up, and hopefully, by the time I'm done, they'll be back."

Ox made his way to the kitchen's cupboard, opening doors until his breathing caught in his chest. He had no idea what he was looking for until he spotted a bag of almond-covered milk chocolate candies poorly hidden behind two cans of baked beans.

With no regard, he tore open the bag, sending the chocolate ovals scattering across the counter and cascading over the edge like a waterfall. Saving what he could, Ox shoved them into his mouth before getting the broom and dustpan from the pantry, sweeping up the rest.

He took the bowl of remaining chocolate into the living room and cradled it while he sat on the fireplace hearth. This was when he would pet Bayou to help him calm down. The biggest parts of his heart were out there.

Maybe I can drive out to the marina? But, what'll that solve?

At least being there would help him feel more useful than standing around here.

He grabbed his jacket and fought to get it on; his hand became wrapped up in the sleeve, and he shook it until he grew dizzy with frustration. The memory of the last time Kate was lost with Matt in the depths of the snow-covered woods returned.

"This is nothing like that," he reminded himself aloud. "And Bayou's already with her."

The inn's phone rang, and Ox's feet first darted left and then right as he found himself trying to remember where he left the phone. His hands matched his feet as the rings continued, and he leaned his head in the direction of the noise.

"This is why we leave the phone on the charger." He groaned and punched the air in front of him, knowing full well he was the one who had lost it.

Ox tossed the pillows around on the couch as the ringing grew louder, then it stopped altogether. Taking one of the fluffy gray pillows, he squeezed it out of aggravation and tossed it toward the sofa like a hot potato.

Suddenly, Ox's cell vibrated in his pocket. He attempted to yank it free, catching the edge of the phone's case on the fabric. He wiggled it side to side until it finally popped loose.

"Hello?" Ox gasped.

"Hey, Ox, it's Richard. Have you heard from Maggie?"

Ox swallowed the lump in his throat, feeling as though it was connected directly to his heart. "Sorry, Richard. Matt and I haven't heard from any of the women. Maggie went out with them on Reese's yacht."

"Shoot. I'll keep trying to call her."

As soon as Ox ended the call, it rang, and he bobbled it in his hand. "Hello!"

"Babe, hi," Kate's voice came through the line. "Sorry, I hope you're not worried. We had a bit of an issue, but I have a signal now. I texted you earlier, but I don't think it went through. We're on our way home."

Ox stood up and straightened his shirt. "Worried? Not at all." He moved the phone away from his mouth and sighed. "It's just good to hear from you. I'm glad you called. I didn't know when to start dinner."

"I think we'll be home in about an hour."

"Great, drive safe."

"I love you."

He smiled. "I love you too."

Ox snapped the cell phone closed as the step to the living room popped under the weight of feet.

"Don't worry, I won't say anything," Matt remarked.

"About what?" Ox smacked the phone on his palm and swallowed hard.

"I was worried about Ali also. However, I'm better at hiding it. Us men need to stick together." Matt made his way toward the couch, and Ox could smell the cedarwood and vetiver cologne he'd lathered on as though it was sunblock. "They can't see us worried."

Ox squeezed the phone in his hand. "I need to call Richard and let him know, and then we get a beer while we wait, nonchalantly, for them to come home."

Chapter 21

Kate shoved the front door to the inn open as Bayou nudged his way past Ali and Maggie, his tail a blur. Before she could set down the bags, Ox's arms wrapped around her, squeezing the air from her lungs.

"I missed you," he whispered into her ear.

"Sorry, we worried you," Kate gasped, trying to catch her breath. "Squeezing. Too. Hard."

Ox released his wife but held onto her biceps as she spotted Richard and Matt coming from the living room.

"Richard?" Maggie stepped next to Kate. "What are you doing here?"

"I was concerned. I hadn't heard from you since last night. Ox let me know that you and Kate were on your way back here." Richard stood in the entryway. "I tried to give you space."

Maggie hurried to him, and they embraced for a few seconds.

Since Kate had very little doubt that Maggie wouldn't come to her senses, her main focus was on the interaction between Ali and Matt.

"Why are you wearing Christmas pajamas?" Ox asked.

Kate glanced down and laughed. "I'll tell you later."

"It's great to see you." Matt stepped closer towards Ali.

"You also." Ali's hair was a flat, dampened mess, and her makeup had all but run off. "Hey, your zit is nearly gone. It must've been the fresh mountain air."

Kate watched with a smirk forming on her lips. *Does everyone who's enamored with each other act like a goof?*

"Yes, mountain air clears the pores." Matt's hand went to his nose. "You strike me as a woman who can take care of herself, an adventurous type."

Kate's eyes squinted, trying to make out Matt's lame flirting attempt as though written on the wall in small print.

Ali adjusted the sunglasses on top of her head. "You're correct. I'm independent and self-sufficient."

Matt shoved his hands into his khaki's front pockets. "I bet if you needed to, you could figure out how to drive a boat without reading a manual."

Kate covered her mouth and smacked Ox on the arm when she heard him snickering. *Is Ali actually falling for this?*

"Possibly." Ali pulled at a strand of her hair with her fingers. "Do you like to be on the water?"

The two were standing close enough they could hug each other without moving an inch.

"Absolutely. I love nature." Matt straightened his stance. "This hike I went on today, the trail had steep and dangerous switchbacks. But I knew if you were with me, you could handle them."

Don't laugh, don't laugh.

"You thought about me?" Ali's cheeks reddened.

Matt reached for his earring and nodded.

"I'm always up for an adventure," Ali purred.

"Great." Matt rocked on the balls of his feet. "Maybe we could go for a hike before the week is over."

"I'd like that." Ali pressed her lips together.

In the kitchen, the timer on the oven beeped. Ox's hand fell from Kate's arm as he went to shut it off. Bayou stood over his food bowl and smacked it with his paw, glaring back at Kate.

"I don't know about everyone else, but Bayou and I are starving." Ox grabbed the potholders and removed the steaming dish from the oven.

After Kate poured the English Lab his kibble and freshened his water, she kissed Ox on the lips. "How did today go without us?"

Ox removed the salad from the refrigerator, and she grabbed the Ranch, Italian, and Blue Cheese dressings.

"Lonely," he said softly. "I did get a phone call, but we can talk about that later." Ox set the serving dish in the middle of the table. "Time for dinner."

"Smells great, Ox." Matt pulled out Ali's chair, and she eased into it.

Ali and Matt gazed at each other without looking away as Matt sat down in the chair next to Ali.

"I think Maggie and I are going to head home. Big day tomorrow," Richard stated with his arm around his soon-to-be bride.

"There's plenty of food. You're welcome to stay." Kate pointed with her hand.

"Thanks for the invite," Maggie said, "and for today, it was exactly what I needed. But it's time to make things right before tomorrow."

Kate nodded. "We can't wait for the wedding."

"We can't either." Maggie rested her head on Richard's shoulder.

The soon-to-be Mr. and Mrs. Madison headed out the front door as plates were served and the side dishes passed around.

Kate poured the merlot, and Ox even had a glass. There was such comfort in being back home, even if the emergency was staged and the storm was real.

Yet, beyond the repose, as they sat around sharing stories from their adventures, she knew Ox couldn't have felt included. Kate reminded herself to be grateful for what they still had together. She blinked at the rambling thoughts of babies and puppies, forcing a smile when Ox glanced at her.

Chapter 22

"Are you sure I have to wear a tie?" Ox groaned as he futzed with the solid blue fabric. "I can't get this." He yanked and then flicked it.

"Yes," Kate asserted. "Just because it's not some fancy church wedding doesn't mean it's not important."

She stood in front of him, wrapping her hands around his tie. "I have no idea what I'm doing. Is there a rabbit and a hole?"

"That's for tying shoes."

Kate located her cell phone on the nightstand and searched for a video. Once she had it pulled up, she returned to Ox, who continued to wrap the tie in knots.

"Here," she handed him the phone, "hold this, please. Did you double knot it?"

She pulled his neck forward as she worked her fingers into the wrapped-up tie's fabric to free it. Once the tie hung straight down around his shoulders, Kate watched the video and followed the steps.

"There." She patted the fabric against his chest.

He looked down and held it between his pointer finger and thumb. "Hey, it's tied."

"Now that we handled the most challenging part of the wedding," he chuckled, "there's nothing we can't do together."

Kate smiled at him and tilted her head.

"What?" Ox asked.

"Nothing, we can talk about it later. We're running late." Kate hurried from the room in her cropped jeans and a gray T-shirt with the sleeves rolled up like Fonzie's shirt.

The fact that Kate hadn't put on her bridesmaid's dress was a good idea. There was an eighty percent chance she'd rip something once it was on.

While he wondered why his wife gave him *the* look earlier, his mind needed to focus on one thing, and that was getting over his apprehension of taking Bayou to the hospital for Leslie's chemotherapy sessions.

The doorbell rang, and it was either the minister or the soon-to-be new-lyweds. Either way, they were not ready or prepared.

Hurrying down the hall, Bayou followed close behind, unsure about all the commotion. Ox's legs were strong today, and he smiled, thinking about not having to use his cane.

As Ox approached the door, rapid little knocks erupted like an angry woodpecker. His brow rose as he swung open the front door.

"Did I miss it? Am I late?" An older woman in a flowing pale dress and shiny dirty blonde ringlets forced her eyes open wide. Her hand pressed against the door's frame, holding a pair of sandals.

"I'm sorry," Ox puffed up his cheeks, "you are?"

She shoved her palm at his chest. "I'm Leah," she hiccupped, "excuse me, Margaret's sister."

"And you've been drinking." He crossed his arms.

"I didn't drive." She spun around, and as she drew her arm out to point, the sandals crashed onto the porch.

"I got taxied in. No," she scooped up her sandals, "I took a taxi. Although I don't think they call them that anymore. Something about a User, no, Usher." Leah's hand waved in the air. "Anyways, I didn't drive. Now, may I please come in?"

Ox opened the door wider as he stepped aside. "Sure, finally someone possibly more clumsy than my wife."

"What?" Leah squinted up at him as though she was looking directly at the sun. "I just need some water. I'll be fine."

Bayou, who'd remained silent at Ox's side until now, let out a low growl in the new guest's direction.

"Bayou, no, it's okay." Ox petted his dog's head.

"Is that the minister?" Kate popped around the corner of the kitchen's entry. "Oh, hi, I'm Kate." She reached her hand out, approaching Maggie's sister.

"Leah." She yanked at her dress.

Kate brought her hand back to her side. "Nice to meet you, Leah. Can I get you some water, or perhaps coffee?"

"Coffee, thank you." Leah lifted her chin at an upward angle as though preparing to meet royalty.

"Come with me." Kate gestured toward the kitchen, her hand hovering near Leah's back.

Once Leah was in front of Kate, she glanced over her shoulder. Her mouth fell open into an O shape. He winced and shrugged his shoulders.

After his wife got Leah set up at the kitchen table with a mug of coffee, she slipped out and met Ox in the hallway with Bayou.

"What a disaster," Ox whispered.

"Maggie did mention she invited her sister." Kate crossed her arms and leaned against the wall. "Can we assume we now know why they aren't close?"

"Sure, assumptions never got anyone in trouble. And while we're at it, we can assume that all chocolate cake is good, when in fact we know that's not true." Ox peered over his wife's shoulder.

"You and the chocolate cake analogy, again."

"The dark chocolate cake of 2019." Ox remembered it as though he could taste the bitterness of it on his tongue.

"Cake aside," Kate pressed her hands together, "how are we supposed to handle Leah?"

"Maggie invited her. There's nothing to handle besides hoping our coffee is strong enough." He gestured with both hands. "And she's dressed for the wedding."

Kate's vision shifted down. "Right, I still need to get dressed. She pulled her cell phone from her pocket. "Oh, shoot. Richard and Maggie should be here —"

The doorbell echoed through the inn.

"Why don't I grab the door, and you get ready." Ox cupped his hands on her cheeks.

Kate was frazzled, and if she didn't calm down, Bayou would be climbing on her to make sure she *became* calm.

But as Kate attempted to hurry off, he grabbed her arm, sliding his other hand around her waist, and pulled her close. He rested his lips against hers, and he felt her body relax as he supported her.

When they parted, Ox gazed down, brushing her coppery curls behind her right ear. "Don't allow Leah being here to ruin the day. It's Maggie's decision, and we'll find out how she wants us to handle the situation."

The doorbell echoed again, and the door creaked open.

"Hello!" Maggie's voice filtered in from the entryway.

As Kate hurried off to the master bedroom, Ox and Bayou headed back toward the front door.

Leah sauntered out of the kitchen, meeting Richard and Maggie in the entryway. Maggie's head shifted from behind Richard as she held a garment bag and a small tote.

"Leah?" Her purse slid from her shoulder.

Richard froze at the sound of Maggie's sister's name, both hands wrapped around bottles of wine.

Ox made eye contact with Richard. "Why don't I take those from you?" He reached out and grabbed them as Maggie and Leah continued to stare blankly at each other.

"You showed up," Maggie proclaimed as Bayou stepped between the sisters.

Leah rested her hands on her hips. "Margaret, it's great to see you. It's been a long time. When I got your invite to the wedding, I couldn't believe it."

"Odd, because I can't believe you showed up here, like this." Maggie's hand pointed, palm up. "I figured you would've known better."

"Better? You mean perfect like you?" Leah moved her foot out as though a kickstand for support.

"No one has ever asked you to be perfect, but at least grow up." Maggie adjusted her purse back over her shoulder.

"Maggie, would you like me to have Leah leave?" Ox stepped forward as Bayou remained focused on the situation at hand, standing between them.

"No, Leah can stay. After all, she came all this way, and she's already dressed for a wedding."

Ox looked at Richard and noticed the helplessness creasing across his forehead.

"Ox, do you mind if I get ready?" Maggie held up the garment bag.

"Not at all. Room four is available for you to use, and I'll send Kate up to assist you. She's still getting ready, but Ali is up there in room two if you need her for anything." Ox set the wine on the kitchen's island.

"Ox, could you help me bring in the cake?" Richard asked.

Maggie made her way up the stairs, and Bayou blocked Leah from exiting the kitchen.

"Bayou, it's okay, come with us." Ox patted his leg.

But the English Lab continued to stare at Leah. The fur on his back rose as his hackles went up.

"Bayou," Ox warned.

The dog's stance eased, and he looked at Ox and then back at Leah.

Maggie's sister pivoted and headed back into the kitchen.

With that, Bayou went to Ox but kept his eyes focused on Leah until she disappeared behind the wall.

This wedding just went from simple to a possible nightmare in less than two minutes.

Chapter 23

Kate's pastel blue chiffon V-neck dress billowed when she emerged from the master bedroom. She was not sure what to expect, but finding Leah in the living room, alone, was not a surprise.

Kate figured Maggie was upstairs getting ready as she spotted the royal blue and lemon yellow cake on the kitchen island. She heard the muffled voices of Ox and Richard out on the front porch — they must be out there hiding from the women.

"Can I get you more coffee?" Kate stepped down into the living room and approached the side of the couch.

She expected to find Leah in tears, or at least with her lips turned down. However, Leah was anything but distraught.

"More coffee would be great." She held out the mug without bothering to rise from the couch and meet Kate halfway.

Kate took a deep breath and removed the mug from Leah's hand.

After pouring more coffee into the cup, Kate set it on the counter.

The cake, three small square tiers, was bigger than she'd expected but beautiful all the same. Each level had a different artistry to it. The blueberry-colored icing appeared like silk as yellow drippings cascaded down from the edges.

As Kate walked in front of the refrigerator to get a closer look at the frosted delight, her bare feet met something wet.

Glancing down, she spotted water streaming out from the bottom of the refrigerator. She turned abruptly and slipped, her arms rotated like windmills, and grabbed the nearest thing her fingers could find.

Kate's left hand raked through the stickiness, landing on the edge of the island, catching herself before her knees hit the floor.

Once stable, she yanked open the drawer of dishtowels and tossed them in the direction of the growing puddle. Then she noticed her left hand, and her heart dropped into her stomach.

"Oh no," she whispered, eyeing the mess of blue and yellow frosting covering her palm.

She glanced at the cake. It looked as though a one-legged cat had tried to scale it.

"No, no, no, no." Kate squeezed her eyes shut.

"What did you do?" Leah's voice came from around the corner.

Kate eyed her. "Don't you say a word."

Leah put her hands in the air as though Kate was about to arrest her. "I'm only here for the coffee."

Kate pointed to the mug on the counter. She had to let Ox know about the refrigerator leaking, but first, she had to fix the cake.

After washing her hands, Kate took a pastry knife from the drawer and mended the claw marks stretching from top to bottom.

Leah had pulled out a stool at the island and watched as Kate worked on the cake, taking loud and lengthy sips of coffee.

Kate stepped back and tilted her head. "Not too noticeable."

"Looks good, kiddo." Leah raised her mug in a toast of agreement.

"As long as no one focuses on the back of the cake, we should be fine." She set the pastry knife in the sink.

The water had soaked through the towels, and she hurried to grab more.

When she returned, Leah's hands braced the front of the refrigerator as though she was trying to pick it up.

"What are you doing?" Kate layered a new set of towels on the floor.

"It's your ice maker. Help me pull it out so you can turn it off."

"Are you sure you can do that?"

"Turn it off? Yes, I'm sure you can. And also, yes, I can help you pull it out. Unless you think I'm too old and weak and you want to make a go of it yourself."

Kate shook her head.

"It rolls, genius." Leah pointed. "Just need to get it started."

Leah got on the right and Kate on the left, and together they wiggled the refrigerator far enough to get a hold of the sides and rolled it out of the alcove.

Kate slipped her arm back behind it. "Where is it at?"

"Are you asking me because I have x-ray vision?"

She rolled her eyes and felt around. Her fingers grazed something that felt like a long knob and turned it. The sound of running water stopped.

"I think I got it." Kate shimmied her arm free.

After Kate mopped up the rest of the water on the floor, she carried the wet towels to the washing machine.

Leaving the laundry room, she noted the change in the room's illumination. It must be getting late. She could break the news about the icemaker to Ox later. Right now, she needed to check on Maggie.

Taking the steps two at a time, Kate rapped on the door to room four. "Maggie?"

"Come in," Maggie's voice called out, barely audible.

Easing the door open, Kate found Maggie sitting on the side of the bed holding a tissue. Her wedding dress was on, but she hadn't done her makeup yet.

Kate hurried to her and lowered herself on the floor, the chiffon spread out in a circle.

"So, Leah." Kate's nose picked up the scent of freesia and jasmine.

"Leah's a train wreck." Maggie took a hold of Kate's outreached hand. "By the way, you look beautiful."

"Thank you. And more like your sister switched onto the wrong track at the railway crossing."

Maggie cracked a half-grin. "You always make me smile. Is she still downstairs?"

Kate nodded. "On her second cup of coffee. Do you want to talk about it?"

Maggie stood and unzipped the small bag resting on top of the dresser. She tilted her head as she gazed into the mirror.

Kate rose and took the spot on the bed that Maggie had occupied.

"Leah's childhood was much more challenging than mine. I'm not sure if you noticed with her arriving as she did, but she has a profound limp from a congenital disability. Children in school were not the kindest to her, and she carried that animosity with her into her adult years." Maggie swiped on tan eye shadow. "Not that she's grown up much."

Kate crossed her arms and sighed. "She overindulges in alcohol because of a limp?"

Maggie applied a coat of mascara to her right eye. "Thankfully, I guess, the drinking started much later in life. Growing up, Leah hid away from the world because of her limp. Slowly, over time, she spent all her time with my parents, mostly our dad, helping him fix everything around the house. When Dad passed away, and shortly after that, our mom, Leah, was lost. I did my best to support her, but she always saw me as our parents' perfect child. In a sense, she sees me as perfect because she never found herself good enough."

"The only person who can help her see herself, is, herself." Kate stood up and watched Maggie in the mirror as she applied mascara to her other eye.

A knock at the door caused them both to look.

"It's Ali," came the voice.

"Come in." Maggie darkened her lips with mauve lipstick.

"What's with the woman downstairs? Her singing is atrocious." Ali's emerald green floral dress fell just below her knees.

"I mean, it's not loud or anything, but it's enough to know she's hopelessly tone-deaf," Ali added as she shut the door.

"That would be my sister, Leah." Maggie shoved the lipstick back into the bag and removed an eyelash curler.

Ali reached for the doorknob. "Should we invite her up?"

"No," Kate and Maggie chorused.

"I'm confused." Ali touched the feather charm on her necklace.

"Leah is here because I invited her." Maggie pushed the handle on the eyelash curler. "Because I'd hoped she'd changed."

"I'd never want anyone in my life that didn't want to be in it." Ali had curled her hair, causing it to appear shorter than usual.

Maggie leaned closer to the mirror. "I love Leah, and she'll always be my sister and in my life to some degree."

"I guess it's a good thing I don't have siblings." Ali went to the open bedroom window.

A breeze of crisp air warmed by the sun pushed through the screen. Maggie turned around and faced them.

"You look beautiful, Maggie." Kate brought her hands to her chest.

"Yes, what a lovely bride." Ali smiled.

"Come here." Maggie held out her arms in a V shape.

Kate grabbed hold of Maggie's soft and slender hand. But Ali was hesitant, and it took Maggie wiggling her fingers to get Ali to finally agree.

"Kate, you know how much I've grown to love you. You're my family, and I'm delighted to share this day with you." She squeezed Kate's hand. "Ali, goodness, it's only been a few days, and your honesty is as unforgiving as sandpaper, but your drive for living life without regrets is admirable."

"What do we do about Leah?" Kate asked as Maggie let go of their hands.

"We do what I've always done." Maggie returned to the mirror. "Hope for the best. For hope is sometimes the only option we have left."

"Speaking of hope." Kate clenched her teeth and attempted a smile. "I hope you'll find it in your heart to not look at the back of your cake. Or cut any pieces from there."

Maggie's face deadpanned. "Kate, what did you do?"

Chapter 24

"Richard," Ox said, "you look sharp."

Richard straightened his posture, and the creases of his tuxedo smoothed out.

"The minister should be here in a few." Ox shooed Bayou's investigative nose away from his black slacks. "I think everything is ready. Please make yourself comfortable. It looks like we're safer staying outside at the moment."

Richard tugged at his black bowtie. "Who would've thought I'd be nervous."

"In that case, let me sneak in and grab us some beers."

The inn hadn't been this chaotic since Valentine's Day when four couples had booked the rooms, and they got in a fight during the romantic dinner. After everyone checked out, Ox and Kate agreed they'd be closed to guests on any future Valentine's Day.

He entered to find Leah in the living room, singing along to Elvis. Hurrying to avoid her, he made a beeline for the kitchen and froze when he noticed the refrigerator was halfway out of the recess.

What? Ox peered around it and scratched at his freshly shaved face. *I'm sure Kate's behind whatever this is.*

He grabbed the beers and dashed out of the kitchen.

Ox returned, popped the top off a bottle, and handed it to Richard, who took a seat on one of the front porch's Adirondack chairs.

"I remember the first time I saw Maggie." Richard took a sip of beer, and Ox lowered himself into the neighboring chair.

Bayou trotted up the patio steps and flopped down with the grace of a watermelon rolling off a countertop.

"At our wedding," Ox inserted.

"Beautiful wedding you and Kate had. Oh, did Maggie ask if Bayou could be the ring-dog? I got a ring for Maggie."

Ox smiled. "No, but of course he can. Wait, I thought you already gave Maggie an engagement ring when you asked her to marry you?"

Richard rested his beer bottle on the armrest. "I told her it was in the spur of the moment, and all I could get was that boring gold band. It's not true. The ring I asked her to marry me with is probably about to turn her finger green."

Richard moved his hand into his pocket and presented an exquisite ring with a ruby in the center flanked by two small sparkling square-cut diamonds.

Ox leaned over and examined it. "She'll love it."

The front door popped open, and Richard slid the ring back into his pocket.

"Those women are having a blast up there." Matt stepped onto the front porch. "They're singing Christmas songs."

"It's July," Richard and Ox said in unison and chuckled.

"What about Leah?" Ox asked.

"Oh, that must be the woman singing off-key in the living room, dancing with a pillow." Matt presented an open bottle of beer in his right hand. "I hope this is pre-vow acceptable?"

Richard raised his beer. "I think anything goes for a wedding as long as the wedding still occurs."

Ox clanked his bottle against Matt's, and Bayou lifted his head at the sound of tires crunching on rocks echoed up the driveway.

"Maggie doesn't have any more siblings, does she?" Ox asked Richard.

"I hope not." Richard brought his beer to his mouth.

"Then that should be the minister, Peter." Ox switched his bottle to his left hand and walked down the steps as a worn and rusted Toyota Camry parked next to Richard's red Chevy truck.

A man in traditional black attire and a white-collar stepped from the car with a Bible in hand. "Hi, you must be Oxnard."

"Please, Ox is fine. Otherwise, I feel like a welcome sign in California." Ox shook his hand. "Nice to meet you, Peter."

"Thank you. It was a delight to receive the call from Richard." Peter spotted him on the porch and waved with his Bible. "To be honest, it's been so long since I last did one of these I was not sure I'd be able to button my shirt all the way up. My wife is a fabulous cook. Or should I say I'm a fabulous eater?"

The men huffed a laugh, and Bayou decided the commotion was getting under his fur and zoomed down the porch steps and sat at Peter's feet.

"This is Bayou." Ox grinned.

"I've heard of the famous Bayou." Peter reached out his hand. "Can you shake?"

Bayou lifted his paw, and Peter took it for a few seconds before letting it go.

"What a good dog." Peter ruffled the top of Bayou's head. "Ox, your inn is mighty impressive. From time to time, folks at church mention it."

"Thank you. You and your wife are always welcome to stop by for a meal or even to spend the night." Ox moved toward the porch, and Peter followed.

"A true delight we'll take you up on." Peter shook Matt's hand and then gave Richard, who stood up, a quick handshake too.

"If you'll excuse me, I should get the final touches ready and find out why my refrigerator is askew." Ox glanced at his watch. "Peter, can I get you something to drink?"

"No, thank you. I'm alright for the moment."

Ox nodded and opened the front door, and Bayou followed. He peeked into the living room as he headed for the kitchen. Leah's back was to him, silhouetted by the sun's setting light coming in through the windows.

Removing a ceramic ivory bowl from the cupboard and a cutting board, Ox diced several tomatoes as his nose reminded his hungry stomach about the ciabatta in the oven.

As Ox plucked fresh basil leaves off the plant near the sink, Leah strolled in. Her walk was steadier than when she arrived, but she had a noticeable limp.

"I thought I heard someone." Leah plunked herself onto the stool at the end of the island. "Do I smell fresh bread?"

"Yes, but it's only for those who behave during the wedding." Ox dripped garlic oil over the top of the tomatoes in the bowl.

Leah laughed. "I'm well behaved."

Ox raised an eyebrow as he removed the ciabatta from the oven with a mitt. "Do you know why my refrigerator is sticking out?"

Bayou continued to observe every move Leah made, and for once in his life, unfazed by the preparation of food.

"Your ice maker busted, and the water ran out from the line. Your wife and I took care of it — temporarily."

"What?" Ox turned to the unit. "It's always something."

A headache formed as he pressed his fingers into his forehead, wondering if this was the start of things breaking around the inn. The washer and dryer were ten years old, and the refrigerator was only three. The weight of responsibility landed on his shoulders like a boulder.

"Do you think I could have a little?" she leaned forward on her elbows and pointed at the bread.

"I think it would be best if we waited. The wedding should be in just a few, and we're running later than planned."

Leah crossed her arms. "I can see why you're friends with my sister. You're a party pooper too."

Ox snickered. "Technically, I'm a wedding pooper."

He relaxed his shoulders, trying to rid the tension from them when the backside of the wedding cake caught his attention.

"Did something happen?" He pointed.

Leah pinched her lips together and shook her head. "I'm not a snitch. I promised your wife."

Before he could respond, the inn's phone rang in the distance, and Ox excused himself to answer it.

"Hello, Inn of the Woods."

Ox didn't bother to sit down. He could quickly add whoever wanted to make a reservation to the calendar and get back to finishing up the summer salad.

"This is Brandon over at the Crooked River Rescue. May I please speak with Ox?"

"Hi, Brandon, this is Ox. What can I help you with?"

"Were you still interested in adopting that chocolate English Labrador?"

Chapter 25

Watching Richard's face warm with delight when Maggie walked out onto the patio with her bouquet in hand would remain in Kate's memory for a long time. However, Kate couldn't shake how distracted Ox appeared, his sapphire eyes darting around as though trying to find an answer he misplaced.

On the other hand, Leah provided more distraction than anything else. She went from examining her nails to heavy sighs and finally to shifting in her chair.

Bayou stood next to Ox and glanced over at Leah every time she caused an interruption. But he looked adorable as a ring bearer with a white ribbon and two rings hanging around his neck.

Peter cleared his throat and continued with the Bible spread open across his hands.

"Excuse me." Maggie turned to her sister. "Leah, do you have an issue being here or with me marrying Richard?"

"Weddings are boring." Leah stood up and yanked at the side of her dress. "I do, I do, blah, blah."

Kate gasped and covered her mouth as all eyes went to her.

"I invited you because I thought this would be a good opportunity to catch up and to see how you're doing." Maggie let go of Richard's hand and stepped forward. "Maybe even mend our relationship."

Leah waved her fingers in the air. "You mean so you can compare your fabulous life to my crappy one?"

A rare growl grumbled from the depths of Bayou's throat.

"You can make your life whatever you want. And I see you made yours into a gigantic pile of crap." Maggie's stance widened.

Redness inched up Leah's neck to her chin as she stepped forward. "I wish you all the bad luck in the world. I hate being your sister."

"That's what makes us different," Maggie choked out, her words filled with tears. "I'm grateful to be *your* sister."

Kate watched as Bayou squeezed between the sisters and raised his hind leg at Leah.

Instantly, the sound of a trickling liquid filled the silence in the air. As though in slow motion, Leah tilted her head down and then screamed.

"I guess Bayou has spoken for all of us," Richard stated.

"Looks like no bread for you, Leah," Ox added.

As Leah stomped off the patio and through the inn, Kate followed her. She locked the door behind her, careful not to let it hit her on the way out. Then she went to Bayou's treat bin, removed a salmon stick, and tossed it to him. He caught it at the edge of his mouth and sucked it in.

"Best dog ever," she announced. "Let's go finish up the wedding. I think you have rings to present."

After the vows, the sunset just beyond the evergreens, providing a glow of oranges and pinks as Richard and Maggie shared a kiss.

However, Bayou was focused on something much more critical as Kate caught him pawing at Ox's leg. Dinner, he needed dinner.

"Thank you all for everything, and my sincerest apologies for my sister ruining everything." Maggie turned to them. "Now, let's eat."

Kate snickered. She couldn't have agreed more. "Alright, everyone, find a seat. Ox and I'll get the food served."

Chair legs scraped against the decking as they pulled out the seats.

"Is everything okay?" Kate asked Ox, walking side-by-side into the kitchen.

Ox removed the bowl from the refrigerator and added a serving spoon. "Yes, why do you ask?"

"You seem distracted." Kate sliced the fresh ciabatta and set it on an oval serving plate. "And you didn't say anything about how I look."

"No." He nodded his head. "I mean, no, I'm not distracted. And you look beautiful. I'm sorry I didn't say anything earlier. The ice maker." He scratched the back of his head. "The ice maker is on my mind."

She couldn't put her finger on it, but something was definitely up, and it wasn't the ice maker. Maybe it was the upcoming therapy with the cancer patient Bayou was going to work with.

"Did you see the way Matt was looking at Ali?" Kate spotted Bayou sitting at his bowl, staring into it like a crystal ball showing future meals.

"Like she was a donut."

"With rainbow sprinkles."

"What's the plan?" Ox asked.

"We need to give Ali and Matt more time alone. The other night was great with the movie and popcorn."

"We need them out of the house and on an adventure." Ox set the wineglasses on a tray.

"What can they do without us? We set everything up as group things."

Kate poured food into Bayou's bowl and gave him fresh water. Bayou drank the water and carried the leftovers in his jowls to the food bowl, making a soupy mess.

"We'll think of something." Ox held the tray.

She followed behind and spotted Matt and Ali sitting next to each other with the sun's light nearly gone.

The scent of flower nectar filled the air as she handed the bread plate to Peter.

Once everyone had food and Ox and Kate were seated, Ox raised his glass. "To Mr. and Mrs. Madison. May their future together be happy and healthy."

They smiled collectively and raised their wine glasses, toasting them with clangs of glass.

"After we finish, we'll enjoy some cake by the fire pit." Kate pointed below the patio. "The front and side pieces only."

Bayou wandered through the French doors and onto the deck. He lowered himself between Ox and Kate, and when she gazed down at him, the thoughts of how lonely he must be lingered.

Soon, she became as distracted in thoughts as Ox had denied only a little bit ago.

Chapter 26

In the late afternoon, after the wedding, Ox made the drive to the rescue shelter and contemplated turning around at least twice. The main reason being the pending divorce request he'd undoubtedly spring upon Kate and the fear that a puppy wouldn't be enough to soften the blow. Yet, every time he ran through what he'd say to Kate, nausea rose in his stomach. It was the last thing he ever wanted to do, but what choice did he have?

He heaved open the shelter's main door, and the sound of barking grew. Bayou's nose went crazy, sniffing every inch of the air and the ground.

"Hi, I'm Oxnard Swanson. I'm here about the chocolate English Labrador."

The woman behind the counter leaned over it. "And who is this?"

"Bayou."

The dog looked up for a brief second and then went back to sniffing.

"He's beautiful. And yes, Brandon said you'd be stopping by for a meet and greet." She walked around and waved her hand. "Follow me."

Ox and Bayou went through a series of doors and ended up in a small, fenced-in grassy area with a bench.

"I'll let him know you're here." She gave Bayou a quick head pat and hurried on her way.

Taking a seat, Ox allowed Bayou's leash to fall as he wandered the playroom.

Soon the door opened, and Brandon entered holding a leash and at the end of it was the chocolate nugget of fur. He was much cuter than Ox remembered, and he understood why Kate had instantly fallen in love with him.

"Hello, Ox." Brandon stretched his hand out, and they shook. "Thanks for coming down and bringing Bayou. We like to make sure any new adoption to a home with other animals is a good match."

"I understand."

"If this works out, we'll do a home visit next." Brandon smiled.

"This is a surprise for my wife. So, if we can work it out without her knowing, that would be fantastic."

"Absolutely." Brandon lowered and allowed Bayou to sniff him out.

Bayou's tail swirled like a helicopter blade, and if the dog didn't weigh so much, he might've taken off.

Brandon dropped the leash and allowed the two dogs to get to know each other.

The puppy romped forward, and Bayou watched with anticipation of what it might do next. In true Bayou fashion, he laid down, allowing the puppy to climb all over him.

"As I mentioned on the phone, the dog was not a good fit for the other family."

"You did, but I had to cut you short and missed why he was not a good fit." Ox watched the dogs chase each other.

"I hope this doesn't scare you off, but the family reported he was a bit much for them, energy-wise."

"They only had him for what, a day and a half? How could they possibly know?" Ox questioned.

"I agree, but we truly want the best home for our adoptions." Brandon rocked on the heels of his sneakers. "It turns out the little guy is obsessed with fetch."

"Obsessed?" Ox tilted his head.

"They had to hide the balls from him. He wanted them to throw the ball or any of his toys non-stop. And when they didn't, he'd whimper and cry."

"Have you had any issues here with him before he was adopted?"

"To be honest, it's hard to say. Most dogs spend their days alone and cooped up, so we usually aren't aware of any such obsessions. The staff thinks the best placement for him would be in a home with another dog that he can play with and burn off his energy, plus someone who's home more often than not. The other couple both worked fifty hours a week, and that's too long for a dog, puppy or not, to be home alone."

"They seem to be getting along fine, and I'd be willing to work with the little guy to make sure he had enough daily stimulation."

"Perfect." Brandon cupped his hands. "It looks like a great match."

Bayou chased the puppy but allowed him to get away every time. Then Bayou flopped down, and his tongue hung out sideways.

"We'll set up the home visit for tomorrow morning if that works?" Brandon asked.

"Yes."

"As long as it goes well, which it should, then the little chocolate fetch freak will be yours tomorrow afternoon."

"Great." Ox smiled. *What could go wrong with a pup labeled a fetch freak?*

Chapter 27

Ox was acting more secretive since the wedding, but Kate had no idea why. It couldn't be about wanting to get another dog because he'd shot that down and didn't even want to talk about it. She said the word sibling, and he'd change the subject like the words were on fire.

Kate knew better than to think she could poke the ox, and as she sipped her morning coffee, she silently scolded herself. Ox had his pride grounded, literally. And she couldn't imagine what it felt like to have something one loved so dearly ripped from their life. Maybe after he started working with Bayou at the hospital, things would change. For now, she'd try her best not to focus on his avoidance. And also, try not to think about the childless feeling trapped in her heart. Thankfully, she had matchmaking with Ali and Matt to keep her busy.

Today, Ox would be taking Bayou to the hospital to help Leslie with her first chemotherapy treatment. And Kate was in charge of figuring out how to entertain their friends until he could join them.

After breakfast, everyone but Kate scurried back to their rooms to get ready for the day. Meanwhile, she moved to the living room and took the time to linger with what remained of her coffee.

Kate gazed at the view of the morning wilderness outside, knowing the importance of taking the time to unwind when Ox was having good days because it gave her the energy and strength to help him on the bad days.

She heard a door upstairs creak open, followed by footsteps down the stairs. When she looked over her shoulder, she spotted Matt's gelled hair.

"Hey," Matt whispered, coming around the couch. "Can I ask you something?"

Kate set her mug on the end table and folded her hands together. "Of course."

He faced the direction of the stairs. "Please don't take this the wrong way, but do you think you could find something else to do for a little bit today? Give Ali and me some alone time?" Matt cracked his knuckles. "I can't show her all the charm I have to offer when I'm competing."

Kate leaned her ear toward him. "Competing? Who are you competing against?"

"No, not like that. More like competing for time. You understand, group conversations versus private conversations."

She nodded. "I hear you. Will do." *This is perfect; he wants to be alone with her.*

Kate's cell phone vibrated, rattling next to her coffee mug. Swiping it up in her hand, she noticed it was a text message from Ali.

Ali: Is Matt with you? I think I heard him leave his room.

Kate: yep

She waved her cell phone in Matt's direction. "It's Ali. Don't worry. I won't say anything to her."

"Thanks, Kate." He nodded and headed back toward the stairs.

When she reached for her mug, her depth perception was off, and she ended up dunking her fingers into the hot liquid.

"Ouch!"

She yanked her hand straight up as her elbow hit the bottom of the lampshade, causing it to wobble. Kate twisted around and caught the lamp before it crashed to the floor.

With a sigh, she secured the lamp back in its spot, grabbed a tissue from the nearby box, and wiped her hand clean.

Footsteps and paw steps filtered down the hall as Kate tried to pick up her mug without dipping her fingers into it again.

"Honey, you're not dressed?" Ox stopped at the living room's landing, and Bayou wandered off into the kitchen. "I thought you'd be ready to go by now."

"Did you not notice I wasn't with you after breakfast . . . in our bedroom?" She laughed at her question.

The doorbell rang, and Ox's eyes widened. He looked at the door and then back to her. Bayou waddled toward it.

"I wonder who that could be?" Kate switched hands with the mug. "Are you expecting anyone?"

Ox rested his hands on his waist. "No, not sure. I'll answer it. You go get ready."

"Ali texted me." She picked up her cell.

"Great, text her back while you get ready."

"But she's right upstairs. Why would I do that?"

"Because she wants to text. Why else would she text you when she's upstairs," he took her hand, "besides, it's the thing to do. Popular, come on, be hip."

"Be hip?"

He gave her a little push down the hall. "Hurry, matchmaking doesn't wait for anyone."

"That's why I need to speak with Ali." She spun around and met his hand inches from her face. "What has gotten into you?"

"Nothing, now hurry, go get your text on. Love awaits!" Ox pointed his finger at the bedroom and hurried around the hall's corner.

"So strange," Kate mumbled and closed the bedroom door.

Maybe Ox's inability to fly was causing him to lose it a bit.

She picked out her clothes, sat on the bed, and sent a text to Ali.

Kate: matt sooooooo likes you

Ali: One of these days, you'll text like an adult with proper punctuations and capitalization.

Kate: no thanks

Chapter 28

"My wife's still here," Ox whispered.

Brandon stood at the front door with the chocolate English Lab on a leash at his side. The puppy's nose moved like a bunny's, and his neck stretched the collar.

Ox ushered them inside as Bayou romped around with excitement. He spun and pounced on all fours, then jumped up like a startled cat and repeated the motion.

"So, this is the famous Inn of the Woods I hear everyone mentioning?" Brandon asked, admiring the entryway.

"Yes, welcome. Bayou, calm down." Ox peeked down the hall, spotting the bedroom door closed. "How long will this take? And do you need to see every room?"

"No, I just need to take a little look around and make sure Bayou is okay with his new baby brother being in *his* home."

Ox rubbed his hands together. "Great."

He knelt and slid his hand under the Lab's chin, giving him a deep scratch. Bayou sniffed every inch of the chocolate's fur, his tail wagging as though it was an orchestra conductor.

Noise from upstairs trickled down as Matt and Ali appeared at the top of the steps.

"Oh my!" Ali declared.

Ox frantically waved his arms in the air as though trying to get a car to halt after darting out into the road. "Shhhhh!" he hissed. "It's a surprise."

Ali and Matt froze on the last step.

"Sorry, but goodness, she's going to love it. Wait, I thought someone else had adopted that dog?" Ali asked.

"No time to explain," Ox fretted. "Can you two handle the inspection with Brandon and Bayou? I'm going to make sure Kate stays in the bedroom."

"We have it covered." Matt smiled.

"Thanks." Ox hurried to the master bedroom.

"Who was at the door?" Kate exited the bathroom, dressed in jeans and a loose-fitting striped T-shirt, with a brush in her hand.

Ox glanced over his shoulder and then back at his wife. "Oh, that was . . . "

Kate's mouth opened, and she stopped brushing her hair. "Was?"

"Was a wrong number," Ox huffed.

"A wrong number at the front door?" Kate tilted her head.

"Wrong, door." He placed his hands on his hips. "Wrong house, door, number."

She squinted at him, shook her head, and returned to the bathroom. He puffed up his cheeks and clenched his teeth.

"Take your time. No rush." Ox held his breath to see if he could hear any noise that might be taking place outside the bedroom's confines.

As he exhaled, Kate peeked around the bathroom door.

"Doing some . . . some lung exercises," he stammered. "It's good to take in deep breaths and hold them."

"Makes sense. Oh, before I forget, be careful with the soap. It's sharp."

Ox rubbed his forehead. "The soap is sharp?"

"Earlier, I slipped in the shower, and it went flying. It took a chunk out of it when it hit the hot water knob."

"I'd love to say that I'm surprised, but we know I'd be lying. So, what's the plan for Matt and Ali today?"

"A little outing that'll allow them to be alone." Kate wedged a baseball hat onto her head, swishing her curls.

A crash echoed from the hall, startling Kate. "Oh, my gosh." She hurried toward the bedroom door.

Ox sprung forward, slapping his palm against the door to keep her from opening it.

"What are you doing?" Kate's hand was on the knob.

"Matt and Ali . . . they wanted . . . they wanted . . . to play tag with Bayou." He continued to push his palm against the door.

Kate's hand fell from the knob. "They don't like dogs. Why would they —"

"I spoke with them and encouraged them to spend more time with Bayou. Really, *really* get to know him."

"And tag inside seemed like a bonding activity?"

"What can I say? MS does weird stuff to my brain." He threw his hands up and then rested one on Kate's shoulders, guiding her away from the bedroom door. "Tell me more about what you have planned for the day."

"We're going to go horseback riding over at Fort Wayne. I'm using the outfitter we usually book for our guests' adventures. And it'll be the perfect way for Ali and Matt to have alone time."

"Sounds promising. What's the plan, exactly?" He sat on the edge of the bed. "I mean in detail, run it past me."

"Ali and I have been to Fort Wayne countless times, but Matt's never been. I couldn't think of a better way for her to see Matt as her knight in shining armor than —"

"On a horse!"

"Plus, there are many perfect spots for a picnic. And an even more perfect time for me to wander off and take photos while they enjoy some alone time." Kate winked. "Ali loves to explore those old bunkers down there."

"Matt, roaming old bunkers? Seems a bit . . . unexotic for him."

"He'll go along with it because he'll want to seem like he loves anything, and he'll want to keep Ali feeling safe in the dark, even if he thinks it's lame. He's a guy, right?"

"A guy? What does that mean?" Ox stood up.

"You know, babe. Men like to be the hero. You're my hero." She batted her lashes.

"I thought Bayou was," Ox stated.

Her hand rested on her hip. "Second place for sure."

Loving her never grew old. Every day he wanted to give her the world. And he only hoped the little chocolate fur ball out in the living room would be enough to make the transition to their divorce easier.

"Did you put on sunscreen?" Ox asked.

"Oh no, I forgot, thank you." She headed back into the bathroom.

"I'm going to go check on things. Make sure you put lots of sunscreen on, and maybe change your clothes again."

"Change my clothes?"

"Yes, your outfit," he ran his hands through his hair, "it doesn't go with a horse."

Before he could hear her response, Ox hurried out the door, down the hall, and arrived in the entryway to find them in the kitchen.

Three of the six dining room chairs were on their backs, or sides and the puppy and Bayou were under the table.

"What happened in here?" Ox inquired.

"They were chasing each other under the table. Bayou doesn't fit as well as the puppy." Brandon lifted a chair off the floor.

"Don't worry about that. Kate's about to finish up and come out here." Ox used his thumb, motioning behind him.

"We're all set. I'll finish up the forms, and have you come by and sign everything about three today?" Brandon squatted and clipped the leash back on the puppy's collar.

Ox nodded his head quickly and smiled. "Thank you."

Brandon gently tugged on the leash to get the puppy's attention, signaling that it was time to go. Bayou watched as though he was taking away his favorite stuffed toy.

"Nice meeting you all." Brandon paused at the door as Ox swung it open. "By the way, great inn. If my wife and I do a stay-cation, we'll give you a call."

"We'd love to have you." Ox smiled.

Brandon waved and headed toward his car as Ox shut the door. Spinning around, he found Kate in the entryway.

"Who was that?" Kate pointed.

Ali and Matt exited the kitchen.

"Girl Scouts. They're all year round now, can you believe it?" Ali asked.

"Really?" Kate adjusted her hat. "What did you order?"

"All of them." Ox grinned.

"Oh, great." Kate beamed. "I'll finish packing up the lunches, and we'll be on our way to today's adventure."

Ox's shoulders relaxed as Bayou met him at the door and whimpered.

"Soon, buddy, I know it's hard to wait," he whispered, scratching behind his dog's ear. "He'll be a part of our family in only a few hours. Otherwise, I'll have to figure out how to order Girl Scout cookies in the off-season."

Chapter 29

"I figured we'd horseback ride near the coastline, enjoy a picnic, and then wander around the bunkers." Kate shut the driver's side door of her 4Runner with her elbow as she pulled her backpack over her shoulders.

"It's a beautiful day for it." Ali looked up at the sky, her hand blocking the sunlight.

Streaks of pure cotton clouds broke up the soft blue of the sky. Waves rolled over the rocks and driftwood along the saltwater shoreline that stretched in both directions. The air smelled of dryer sheets made from candy. Kate's mouth watered when she spotted a food truck with photos of sweets plastered on the side of it.

Beaten down dirt paths through the grasses lead to the system of catacomb bunkers and gun batteries from the late eighteen-nineties. Massive doors with rivets the size of quarters were open, flanked by steep short steps. The gigantic cannons remained mounted to the metal mounts drilled into the circles of concrete. Groups of kites dipped and fluttered in the wind. The strings were controlled by the people standing in the open fields between them and the white and black lighthouse.

They were meeting Ernest in the parking lot on the top of the bluffs, and when Kate noticed him pulling in, she gave a wave.

"Kate, great seeing you again," Ernest said as they approached the horse trailer. "Nice to meet you both. I'm Ernest."

Ali shook hands first. "I'm Ali."

"Matt," he shoved his hand at Ernest.

"Kate, let me know you're not newbies, so it'll be a great day to ride and relax." Ernest undid the latches to the trailer.

While Ernest worked to unload the four horses, Kate made sure the ice in the cooler hadn't shifted in the back of the 4Runner.

Once Ernest had saddled up Ali and Matt's horses, he helped Ali up onto her horse, and Matt followed.

It'd been a few years since the last time Kate rode, but she was confident she could remember enough to help Ernest saddle up the horse she'd be riding.

"Let me help with mine." Kate tossed the blanket over the horse's back, followed by the saddle.

Then she adjusted the length of the stirrups. Stepping up onto the block, Kate wedged her boot into the stirrup as she grabbed hold of the saddle horn. With a big pull, she heaved her right leg up, but it was at that moment she realized she'd forgotten one crucial part, synching down the girth strap under the horse.

The saddle rotated from the horse's back to under his belly. Then, still holding tight to the saddle horn, Kate swung around, landing with a thump onto the block.

Ernest came running over and helped her to her feet.

"Kate, you never synched the girth strap." Ernest removed the saddle and blanket and then properly added them back, synched correctly.

"I did forget." She brushed off her bottom and placed her hands on her knees, taking in a deep breath.

"I bet you won't ever again." Ernest raised his eyebrows. "Are you okay to get back on?"

Kate's back cracked when she arched it.

"Of course." She shoved her foot in the stirrup. She did a little bounce to make sure the saddle wouldn't whip around again and cleared her right leg over, finally on top of the horse, instead of under it.

Ali was still laughing when Kate looked over at her and Matt.

"Don't think I forgot about the time when you almost decapitated yourself, Ali," Kate warned.

"What?" Matt slid on his classic black Wayfarer-style sunglasses.

Ali, dressed in dark leggings with taupe ankle boots and two-layered tank tops, shook her head. "It's nothing."

"I must hear this story." Matt adjusted himself on the saddle.

The brim of Kate's baseball cap caught the wind, and she yanked it tighter onto her head. "Back when we were teenagers, Ali and I went horseback riding on this mountain trail. The night before, there'd been a storm, and it left branches all over the place. Ali was too stubborn to listen to the guide, so she took off with her horse. As she went around a switchback, she discovered the broken limb of a tree inches from her face. Thankfully, she ducked just in time."

"See, not a big deal at all." Ali held the reins loose in her hands.

"I'm glad you still have your head." Matt grinned.

"Are we ready?" Ernest turned his horse in the direction of the path with a squeeze of his right leg.

One by one, they entered at the trailhead, and as they rode further on the path, they spread out, allowing the horses to trot. The well-beaten trail from centuries of riders kept the trees and foliage at bay, allowing for breathtaking views.

Ernest's horse and Kate's horse kept in time with each other, leaving Matt and Ali separated enough from them to feel somewhat on their own.

Kate focused on the horse's rhythm as its hoofs pounded against the ground. The scent of cedar mixed with the salt off the nearby water. If she didn't need to remain upright, falling asleep would be easy with the gentle gallop of the horse.

They followed the six-mile trail as it looped around Fort Wayne and back to the parking lot.

Kate watched Matt help Ali off her horse, his hands outstretched around her waist as she swung her leg over. Once safely on both feet, Matt's hands remained on her waist, and Ali's face was in line with his. Matt was only a few inches taller than Ali, but she did have a bit of a heel on her boots.

Slowly Matt's hands fell from Ali's waist, and he shoved them into his jean pockets as though if he didn't, he'd never let her go. They said something to each other, but Kate was not close enough to hear what was said.

Seeing them caused Kate to miss Ox, and she wished he'd been able to come with them. But Bayou's work was important not only to her husband but also to the residents of Crooked River.

A part of her was glad he could no longer fly, even though she would never tell him. Every time Ox took his Cessna up, she seemed to find herself holding her breath off and on until he called to let her know he'd safely touched down. Kate only wished it was not MS that caused his dream to end. Her selfish need for his safety was not worth his unhappiness.

"Kate?"

Ernest stood ready with the block for her to dismount. She refocused on the present and spotted Matt and Ali by the 4Runner.

"Thank you for this." Kate straightened her shirt after she landed on the ground, this time with her feet. "I had a lot of fun. Are you hungry? I brought plenty of food."

Ernest removed the saddle from the horse. "Thank you for the invite, but I have another booking over in Redwood at two."

"Well, in that case, thank you for your time." She removed the keys from her backpack.

"You're welcome. I hope you and your husband can book an adventure before the end of the year." Ernest hung the blanket on a hook inside the trailer.

"I'll see what we can do to make it happen. We haven't been on a date in months." Kate's heart twisted in her chest. "Have a great rest of your day. Thank you again."

Ernest gave her a half-wave and returned to load up his trailer as she made her way to the 4Runner.

"We're starving." Ali pushed her sunglasses up like a headband.

Matt nodded. "I don't even care what you packed. I'll eat it."

"I always wonder what it is about riding horses that makes everyone so famished." Kate popped the hatch.

Ali snatched up the large blue quilt they'd used for their women's yacht getaway, and Kate handed Matt the bag with the serving ware and drinks.

After locking up the vehicle, Kate led them to a spot just west of the bunkers. There was a view of the sound near the edge of the bluff where they could watch the ferry come and go, but still far enough from the children running around and people flying kites.

Ali shook the quilt open, and Kate caught the side of it.

"Remember when we did those parachute games in gym class?" Ali lowered her side of the quilt to the grass. "I remember tossing those balls on it and shaking it, so they popped up into the air."

Instantly the memory of the rainbow-colored fabric flooded into her thoughts.

"I remember them smacking me in the face when they landed." Kate set her side down and knelt on it.

"It was as though nothing bad could ever get to you when we were under there." Ali lowered onto the quilt.

"I loved running under it. The colors were like a kaleidoscope of happiness." Kate sighed. "Sometimes, I miss being a kid."

Matt removed a can of rosé from the bag and wiggled it in Ali's direction.

"Except when the wine comes out." Ali beamed and snatched it from his hand.

Matt sat down next to Ali and crossed his legs. Kate unclipped the old-school picnic basket.

"Chicken salad sandwiches." She handed a wrapped package to Matt and Ali and set one in her lap. "I also packed chips."

Presenting the mini-chip bags, Ali was the first to grab the sour cream and onion flavor.

"Is everything alright, Kate?" Ali unwrapped her sandwich. "You seem more distracted than usual."

Kate shook her head and bit into the bread. Placing a napkin over her mouth, she mumbled, "I'm great."

While she would open up to Ali, she wasn't about to do it in front of Matt.

Chapter 30

Bayou yanked on the leash left and then right as they entered the pet supply store. Removing the list from his pocket, Ox reviewed it.

"We probably need a cart, buddy." He backtracked toward the door and pulled one from the line-up.

It'd been a while since Ox had taken Bayou to a pet store, and as the dog guided him like the leader of a dog sled team, he regretted he'd waited so long.

"If you're this excited about being here, we can come more often." Ox allowed Bayou to steer him down an aisle.

The shelves were stocked full of stuffed toys, ropes, and an assortment of balls. "Good thing your brother isn't with us. I heard he has a thing about fetch."

Bayou shoved his head into every bin of toys, sniffing around.

"We can get a few new toys, but you'll need to share them."

A chirp at the end of the aisle caught the dog's attention, and suddenly Ox was going forward as Bayou tugged on the leash.

He led them to a clear case allowing for a view of the birds, and the English Lab's tail swung back and forth like a hammock in the wind. Bayou pressed his nose up to the case and then sat, his tail sweeping the floor behind him.

A woman in a stroller with a toddler kicking its feet pulled up beside Ox.

"Sometimes, I think dogs and little ones have a lot in common." The woman turned the stroller to face the bird case, and the child kicked its feet and squealed out, "Ird!"

"She can't say her B's yet." The woman leaned on the stroller's hand bar.

"In that case, I'm afraid my dog's name might sound like Pig-Latin." Ox watched as Bayou and the toddler continued to observe the birds.

The woman pulled out her cell phone. "As a parent, I have to take breaks whenever I can get them."

"I can only imagine how much work children are, but I'm sure they're worth it." Ox waved at the little girl.

"I could say the same thing about dogs. My brother has two, and they keep him busy." The woman looked down at her cell phone. "We're here for a fish."

A bulldog entered the store and directed its owner toward the aisle with the bones. Bayou caught a glance at the newest customer and decided the birds were no longer worthy of being watched.

As they wandered down the aisle to follow the dog, Bayou's nose discovered pure delight. He sniffed a long amber bone and then sat, whimpering.

"Great selection." Ox placed it in the cart.

Bayou spotted the bulldog and began walking toward it.

"Is your dog friendly?" Ox asked the older man holding the leash.

The gentleman turned to Ox. "Of course, he loves to meet new friends. Say hi, Albert."

Ox allowed for slack in Bayou's leash, and the two greeted each other with a few sniffs.

At Bayou's height, he towered over Albert, and the bulldog took advantage of the opportunity and tried to shove his way under the yellow Lab.

Bayou returned the advance by doing what he did best, laying down.

Albert snorted a bark, and Bayou eased back up onto all fours.

"Come on now, Albert, we have more errands to run."

Ox nodded with a smile and returned to his shopping list as Bayou whimpered, trying to follow Albert and his owner down the aisle.

"Soon, buddy, you'll be a big brother, just a few more hours."

He gripped Bayou's leash tight as he stood back from the hospital's sliding doors. Every time they opened, the smell of lemon and bleach waffled out, irritating Ox's nose.

"I don't know, Bayou." He wrapped the leash tighter around his hand.

"Ox? Bayou?" A voice came from behind him.

He pivoted around to find Victoria and Leslie coming up the sidewalk. *Crap! No way to turn back now.*

"I'd recognize Bayou anywhere," Victoria chimed as she approached.

"Are you ready?" Victoria looked at Ox and Leslie.

Leslie didn't showcase a willingness to go inside either.

The door slid open again, and out walked a young couple, the woman clearly pregnant as she held her belly. Instantly Ox missed his wife. She was stronger than he was with a lot of things. Maybe Kate should be Bayou's new therapy instructor, and he could do anything but *this*.

"What do you think, Bayou? Are you ready?" Victoria wedged her hands between her knees and lowered herself to the dog's eye level.

Bayou looked at her and then Leslie, but Ox held tight to the leash as though it was his safety line, preventing him from leaping.

The dog sat and leaned on Leslie's legs. She reached down and rested her hand on his head.

Ox unclenched his jaw. "I guess I won't ever be ready."

Leslie's lips parted. "I think we're all nervous, but with Bayou's help, I — we just might make it through."

Ox couldn't have said it better himself. Yet, as he gave the leash to Leslie, a slight tremor shook his hand and traveled up his arm. He placed his opposite hand on his forearm and squeezed it.

They entered through the hospital doors, each with their own hesitations.

Chapter 31

"Kate, can I steal you away for a minute." Ali rose from the quilt. "Matt can fend the flies off by himself."

Reluctantly Kate followed Ali to the bluff's edge, both of their backs to the picnic spread. She didn't want to whine or acknowledge her remorseful feelings towards the decision not to have children. So what if sometimes seeing families caused her to ponder what would've been if her husband didn't have MS. But, life was not perfect.

"I don't want to talk about it, and I most definitely don't want to make a list," Kate warned. "Should I mention how cute you and Matt are together?"

Ali crossed her arms. "Don't try and change the subject."

"Matt's only here for a few more days." Kate turned to her best friend. "Time's a-wasting."

"You oxymoroned yourself." Ali tucked her hair behind her ear. "He's leaving, and you want me to explore a relationship?"

"I thought I was leaving when I started to fall in love with Ox. Plus, I know you find him to be a — how did you put it — a manly ocean."

"He's attractive if you like men to be good-looking." Ali glanced at her boots as her cheeks blushed. "He's one of those guys."

"One of whose guys?"

Ali bit the corner of her lip. "The kind who think they want to settle down but don't actually want to."

"You don't want to settle down either."

"Tell me how a relationship with two people who don't want to settle down would work then?"

"I bet there's an app for that."

"It's all of them, all the dating apps, except for Love Over 70."

"If *that's* an actual app, I don't want to know why *you* know about it." Kate observed two kites, rainbow-colored, battling in the wind. "Wouldn't it be nice to share your adventures with someone?"

"As I said on our girls' day, I like my adventures solo. A one-woman band."

"A band by definition is a group. And you can't play any instruments."

"Then I'm an artist exploring my world, alone."

Kate lifted her sunglasses to her forehead. "See my eyes rolling? I wasn't sure if you could see them. Look." She pointed as she drew them up toward the kites. "Why don't I take my lunch to go? I have so many photos around here I've wanted to take."

"Leave him and me, alone, together?" Ali reached out for Kate's arm.

"You've been alone with him before. Plus, I don't think he'll bite unless you ask him to." Kate turned around. "Hey, Matt, you don't bite, do you?"

"Kate," Ali screeched, hurrying after her.

"Why would I bite?" Matt's face scrunched up at the brows.

"We were chatting about how flies can bite." Ali lowered herself onto the quilt, sitting on her knees.

"Flies do bite. It hurts more than you'd think." Matt rubbed at his arm.

Kate collected her sandwich, drink, and camera off the blanket. "I'm going to get some . . . fresher air. You two have fun."

Navigating the slight dips in the field of grass, Kate located a single bench. It faced the water, and if she tried hard enough, she could easily confuse it for the coast of Ireland she'd seen in those giant coffee table books.

She removed the rest of her sandwich from the wrapper and bit into it as though it was delicate finger food. Three bites in, a glob of chicken salad toppled from the bread and landed smack dab on the zipper flap of her jeans.

"Oh no, mayonnaise stains." Kate used a pincer grasp to pick up the piece when out of the corner of her eye came a bright rainbow pattern.

A gust paired with a woosh brought the pattern to a crash at her feet. She squealed and leaned back. However, she forgot the bench was backless.

Kate toppled backward, landing with a thump on the ground. The sandwich, which she'd flung straight up, came down and busted open on her chest.

She sighed and readjusted her baseball hat. "I'm so over this day."

"Sorry, lady!" A kid about ten years old called out as he dashed to pick up the kite. "Are you okay?"

"I'm fine, thank you." Kate pushed herself up onto her elbows.

"Okay, good." He snatched up the kite and hurried off.

Pushing herself further upright, a toddler wobbled by with a couple right behind him. The toddler toppled when his feet went much faster than expected. Kate watched as the dad came up behind him, swung the child up in the air, and kissed his cheek.

Kate didn't feel it come on, but she knew why as her eyes filled with tears. It had nothing to do with wearing her lunch or being flat on her back for the second time today.

Even though she and Ox had decided not to have kids, it didn't make it easier to overcome societal expectations. Growing up, she always assumed she'd be a mom and never thought anything different. A woman is supposed to be a mom. At least that's the guilt she felt in her heart; it's wrong if you don't have a typical family. The notion suffocated her. She only wished she could stop her mind from spinning around the thoughts haunting her. It was causing Kate to feel as though she wasn't enough of a woman without being a parent.

She needed to talk to Ox about it, but she worried he'd take the blame. The decision to not have children was the right one for them, even if it hurt. She just needed to understand if she'd ever get past it.

Trying her best to focus, Kate gathered up the sandwich pieces and tossed them into the open garbage bin. Then she removed a wet wipe from her backpack and cleaned as much as she could from her T-shirt and pant's zipper.

As she tossed the dirty wipe into the garbage next to the bench, she peeked over at Matt and Ali. They were sitting close together, and Matt kept touching Ali's arm. Kate could see Ali's hand near the base of her neck, no doubt running her charm back and forth on the necklace's chain.

Raising her camera to her eye, Kate zoomed in and snapped a few photos. If Matt and Ali did form a relationship, they'd have a nice picture of their first picnic together.

Chapter 32

While Ox wasn't exactly sure what to expect, it seemed as though Leslie and Bayou's first session had gone well. The dog responded without hesitation to the hospital environment and picked up on Leslie's anxiety, especially when they brought out the needles.

"Great job today, Bayou." Ox lifted the back end of the dog into the truck and checked his watch. "I'd stop and get you a special treat, but we're running late."

Bayou glared sideways at Ox, showing off the whites of his eyes as his right eyebrow arched toward the sky.

The dog was trying to let Ox know he'd be the saddest dog ever if they drove past the Dairy Queen without stopping for a treat.

Ox re-checked his watch. "Okay, but only if there's not a line at the drive-thru."

Bayou sat up straight as if to say: *Darn straight we're going to the DQ.*

Once the ice cream cone was gobbled up, and Ox cleaned the sticky mess of drool off the armrest, he sipped the last of his strawberry shake. By the time Ox parked the truck in the shelter parking lot, only two cars were left.

Bayou slept at Ox's feet as he signed the final paperwork, and the little brown English Labrador came trotting in on his leash as though he knew what this afternoon meant.

"I still can't believe they gave back the dog." Ox set the pen down.

"Adopting an animal can be a lot like fostering a child. Of course, we always hope for a good match, but until the family has time to get to know each other, it's hard to say." Brandon stapled the papers together and filed them into a drawer. "And between us, I don't think the other family gave the little guy enough of a chance."

"Well, he has a family with us, no matter what." Ox stood and took hold of both dog's leashes. "I can't wait to see my wife's face light up."

However, the drive home tested Ox's patience and possibly Bayou's as well. For a third time, Ox pulled the truck over into the gravel on the side of the road.

"Buddy, you've got to calm down." Ox turned around and faced the back seat.

Bayou was sitting calmly on his designated side, but the puppy had twisted himself up in his seatbelt.

During the drive, the chocolate fur ball kept lunging between the front seats. But since Ox had seat-belted him into a harness, he could only go so far.

"You can't sit up here. It's not safe." Ox petted him on the head and then gave a few head pats to Bayou to make it equal.

Continuing with his wiggle fest, the puppy wrapped himself up and flopped on his back, kicking his paws in the air. Ox reached over the armrest, unsnapping the seatbelt from the harness as the puppy flipped over, free at last.

He licked Ox's face and remained standing, panting with delight. As Ox twisted back around, he rested his hands on the steering wheel.

A thump hit the armrest, followed by two giant chocolate paws and a drooling tongue. The puppy's back legs scrambled, lifting him between the front and back seats. With one last wiggle, the puppy cleared the armrest and was promptly in the passenger seat.

Ox pressed his tongue against the front of his teeth and glanced over to see the puppy sitting upright in the seat. He swore it looked like the dog was smiling.

"So, I guess you're sitting up here."

The puppy tilted his head as if to say: Yes, I am.

"Fine, but you need to be buckled in. It's safer for you in the backseat, although I have a feeling it'll take me hours to get home if I don't allow you to be in control."

Ox worked the seatbelt through the harness's designated loop in the back and snapped it into place.

Setting his hand back on the steering wheel, Ox waited. He wasn't going to pull back onto the road if the puppy decided to act erratically again. But the little chocolate fur ball remained calm.

"Well then, I guess you're going to be my shotgun rider." Ox put the truck into drive and pulled back onto the road.

When the three of them arrived home, he parked his truck alongside his wife's 4Runner in the garage.

The puppy hadn't let out a single whine the rest of the way home. And at one point, he curled up on the passenger seat and rested his chin on the outstretched hand of his new owner.

"You're going to be a snuggler, aren't you?" Ox shut off his truck.

The puppy's hazel eyes questioned everything around him as his pupils dilated. Ox wrapped his arm around the dog as though he was a stack of logs he needed to haul inside.

"We just need to come up with a name for you." Ox opened the back door, and Bayou fumbled out with his usual amount of grace.

Instead of making his way to the inn, Bayou peered up at the puppy, sniffing and hopping on his back feet.

"You're not a kangaroo. Come on, let's go surprise Kate."

With each step toward the front door, Ox hoped his wife would be delighted with the new addition. Sure it wasn't a baby, but if this dog was the hyper ball-loving animal the other family claimed him to be, it might be just the distraction they both needed.

Chapter 33

Kate diced up the mushrooms and scooped them into the bowl when the sound of Bayou's paws scampered into the kitchen. In the distance, the front door banged shut as she rinsed off her hands.

"Hi, buddy. Did you have fun today?" Kate knelt and grabbed hold of Bayou's face, rubbing at the side near his ears.

When she stood, Ox was at the kitchen's threshold, with his back turned to her.

"Ox, what are you doing?" She laughed, returning to the pot of boiling potatoes on the stove.

But he didn't turn around. "I have a surprise for you." He appeared to be holding something, but she couldn't see his arms.

Bayou hurried back to Ox, staring up at him.

"A surprise! Let me see." Kate set the spoon on the counter and made her way to her husband.

"Wait!"

She paused in her steps. "What's going on?"

"Close your eyes. I didn't plan this well at all."

Kate giggled as she covered her eyes with both hands. "Okay, they're closed and covered."

She listened for his footsteps as they drew near. Thoughts of what it could be raced through her mind. Maybe flowers, but her favorites were already growing out front. Perhaps it's the new release novel from one of her favorite authors, Rachael Bloome.

"Hold out your hands," Ox instructed.

"This isn't going to be like the time you surprised me with a giant frozen turkey after I forgot to put the order in?"

"No, this is not nearly as frozen, but it's as heavy, if not heavier." His voice was closer.

She stretched out her hands and then pulled them back to her sides. "I'm scared."

"Don't be."

Kate groaned and eased her hands back out, wiggling her fingertips with anticipation. Bayou's hopping could be heard just below her.

She turned her face away, suddenly afraid of whatever was about to happen.

"Keep them closed," Ox said.

She felt the air around her arms change as whatever it was nearly touched them.

Something profoundly heavy and wiggly but warm and furry rested in her arms as she wrapped her body around it. Before Ox could instruct her, Kate opened her eyes to find an overly handsome chocolate English Labrador puppy resting in her arms.

"Oh, my goodness!" Kate squealed. "Oh, goodness, goodness!"

She pressed her cheek against the puppy's ear as instant tears formed. "Who's this?"

"He doesn't have a name yet." Ox smiled.

"Wait, this looks like the dog at the Fourth of July celebration."

"It is."

"But, I don't understand?" She continued to hold the puppy even though her arms were aching from the weight.

"I stole him."

Kate nearly dropped the furball. "What?" The words caused her heart to sink into her toes.

"I know how much you wanted a puppy, and there wasn't another one in the entire world. So, I figured how hard could it be to steal a dog?" Ox shrugged and motioned to the puppy. "Ta-da!"

"Oxnard," she pressed the dog to her chest, "you can't do that."

He smiled wide. "Of course I didn't — don't be ridiculous."

She sighed and snuggled the dog more. "So what happened?"

"Long story, but let's just say we might be able to get our fitness trackers to an entirely new step count if we strap them on him."

As she beamed with joy, her heartbeat pumped rapidly against the puppy who'd set a front paw on either side of her shoulders and licked her face.

Tears continued to trickle down as emotions swept through Kate and her arms burned from holding the squirming addition to the family.

At the moment, Kate felt complete but couldn't help but wonder if the joy of bringing a child home had the same reaction. And sadly, Kate allowed the thought to overshadow the true joy she felt about the puppy.

Chapter 34

After they cleared dinner plates from the table, Kate drove over to her parents with Bayou and the pup, leaving Ox with Matt and Ali.

"I thought it'd be a great night to enjoy some wine on the back patio." Ox offered. "Kate shouldn't be gone too long."

"I hope you plan on making her a snack for later tonight," Ali warned. "She barely touched her food. She was too busy cuddling the puppy."

Ox beamed, thinking about how much Kate loved the newest family member. "Yes, hopefully, his need for attention won't last forever. Or should I say Kate's desire to smother him constantly?"

He pumped soap into the sink's water. "Why don't you both take advantage of the evening? I'll bring the wine in a minute. I want to get these pans soaking."

Matt and Ali headed outside, and suddenly the inn's kitchen felt cold and lonely. With his wife, Bayou, and the new pup gone, it didn't feel like someplace he wanted to be for long. *How am I ever going to get divorced?*

Since the first time he met her, nothing he did felt correct or complete if she wasn't there with him. Like a house with plastic covers on the couch. What mattered was what was under the plastic.

With the pots soaking, he grabbed the bottle of chardonnay and two glasses, spotting Matt and Ali outside leaning on the rail. They were standing close enough to each other that no light came between them. Ox found himself stopping to watch for a second before stepping through the open French doors onto the patio.

Matt turned around, but Ali remained focused on the view.

"Thank you." Matt took the glasses from him and set them on the outside table.

"I almost forgot. I picked up some wonderful white chocolate to have with this wine. It pairs nicely."

"White chocolate?" Ali spun around. "You and Kate *do* have a lot in common."

"What? This chardonnay is supposed to pair nicely with white chocolate." Ox started to pour the wine into the glasses. "You don't like white chocolate?"

"No," Matt and Ali said in unison.

"What's not to like?" Ox asked.

"It's overly sweet." Ali took a glass of wine from Ox. "Not to mention the chalky aftertaste."

"Caulk covered in powdered sugar," Matt added.

"Shall I bring out milk chocolate?" Ox studied their expressions.

Matt and Ali looked at each other.

"Dark chocolate?" Ox poured Matt's glass of wine.

"Yes," they responded.

"Now that's a no for me. Dark chocolate is as bitter as a bad grapefruit." Ox shook his head as he went inside to find the small stash he had in the pantry for guests only.

"Here you go, you crazy kids." He handed off the small dish of assorted wrapped dark chocolates to Matt.

"I'll leave you two to chat." Ox left the wine bottle on the patio table and headed inside.

He picked up the remote, switched on the television, and located an episode of *Friends*. But it was like he was watching a tennis match, keeping one eye on the show, and one eye on Matt and Ali. Kate would want a play-by-play when she got home.

The sun had dipped low enough behind the tree line that it illuminated the sky like layered swatches of blue paint. Matt and Ali had taken a seat on the swing facing the view. They took turns looking at each other as they sipped wine and unwrapped the chocolates.

From what he could see, they appeared to be getting along. Yet, he needed to do something to make it more romantic for them. He could select the perfect set of pajamas or cook up a great meal. However, the cupid-style romantic ambience was Kate's forte.

The laughter and chatting carried on, and Ox reached for the remote, putting the show on mute.

I'm only eavesdropping because I need to report back to Kate.

Glancing around the living room, he spotted a blanket. *Blankets are cozy and romantic.* He snatched one up and headed to the patio.

"Just in case you two get cold." Ox handed Matt the blanket.

"Thank you, it was getting a little chilly," Ali said.

"Oh, you were cold? You should've said something. I could've gotten you a blanket," Matt asserted.

"I didn't want to interrupt our conversation," Ali responded.

Matt laid the blanket across both of their legs. "Me either."

She blushed and brought her wine glass to her mouth as though trying to hide a flirtatious smile.

"Can I get you two more wine or something else to eat?" Ox offered.

"More wine would be great." Ali held up her glass which was about a quarter full.

Ox snatched the bottle off the table and brought it to her.

"Probably best to keep it next to you," Ox suggested. "You know, for drinking, to keep drinking, top it off." He stood up straighter. "I'm going to go back to the living room now."

And *that* was why Kate was the matchmaker.

Chapter 35

She knocked on her parent's front door as Bayou used the opportunity to investigate the front yard. The puppy yanked Kate's arm in the opposite direction, trying to explore the front porch at the end of his leash. When Bayou finished, he clomped up the steps just as the door swung open.

"Sweetheart," Kate's mom cheered. "Oh, who's this?" She reached her hands toward the English Lab.

"Meet the newest Swanson." Kate's body snapped forward, and her head whipped back as the puppy lunged toward her mom.

"Gene!" Josie called out. "We have a granddoggie!"

Kate dropped the leash and followed her mom inside. Josie was already at the steps down to the den with the puppy wiggling in her arms.

"Mom, don't carry him! He's too heavy for you!"

Once Bayou was inside, Kate shut the door.

"A grand what?" She heard her dad call out as she hurried after her mom.

Kate's flip-flops sunk into the plush carpet as she headed down the steps that matched Bayou's fur. "Hi, Dad."

He was sitting in his recliner watching an episode of *Coach*.

"Gene, look." Josie held out the puppy as her dad kicked the footrest into the recliner, sitting him upright.

"You got a new dog?" Dad asked.

"I love that you refer to animals like furniture, Dad. He's not a new coffee table. He was a surprise from Ox." Kate sat down on the couch wedged next to the recliner.

Bayou squeezed his way between Josie and Gene as if to say: New puppy or not; I'm still your number one grandpup.

"What's his name, Kate?" Josie set the wiggle-worm on the carpet.

"He doesn't have one yet." *Please don't tinkle on my parent's floor.*

"How has Bayou done with him so far?" Gene looked the dog over as though he was inspecting a used car.

"So far, good. Minus the drive over. He's not a fan of the back seat. Anyway, I know he and Bayou spent time together during the adoption process. Ox took him to the shelter, and there was a home visit that happened right under my nose." Kate slumped forward.

"I love you already," Josie gushed, sitting on her heels.

Tears welled up in Kate's eyes. She knew how badly her parents, at least her mom, had wanted to be a grandparent. And as an only child, Kate was their only hope.

"I'm sorry," Kate bawled and covered her face. "I'm sorry."

"Josie, why don't you take Bayou and the new dog upstairs for a treat? I want to talk to Katie," Gene suggested.

Without hesitation, Josie hurried up the stairs, with Bayou and the puppy on her heels.

Through watery eyes, Kate glanced around the den. It hadn't changed since her childhood. Wood paneling covered one wall while the other walls were painted a creamy white and held mismatched framed family photos, her father's service awards from the Army, and Grandpa's folded-up flag was positioned in the middle.

"I know, Mom, and you want grandkids. I mean ones that you can bounce on your knee like Grandpa used to do with me." Kate grabbed a tissue from the coffee table and blew her nose. "You can't bounce a dog."

"Katie." Gene sat back in his chair and folded his hands together, his elbows rested on the armrests. "What your mom and I want shouldn't be held in high regard to the life you want and have with Oxnard. We love you both, and whatever type of family you make, be sure it's for you. Your mom is equally equipped to spoil dogs as she is a baby. The future of Oxnard's MS is uncertain, and we're all aware of that, but the one thing we want is for you to have zero regrets. Because, Katie, *that* would be the biggest mistake you could make."

She closed her eyes and leaned back into the plushness of the couch, allowing it to engulf her. The pounding of feet running around above them caused Kate's eyes to stare at the ceiling. She didn't know what to say to her dad, yet she knew it was okay to sit there and not say a word.

Chapter 36

The front door creaked open in the distance, followed by the stomp of boots and paws scrambling towards the living room. *I still have to oil the door.*

"How's it —" Kate started but stopped as she leaned over the back of the couch. "Are they . . ."

"I think they might," Ox whispered and stood to get a better view.

The puppy might have wanted to play with Bayou, but the yellow furball had only one thing on his mind: Find Matt and Ali.

After a few sniffs around the couch and then in the air, Bayou's nose directed him on a new course.

"Bayou," Kate whispered. "No, Bayou, come here."

Ox patted his knee. "Bayou, come."

But the dog knew it was a trick and ignored them.

Bayou followed the scent to the French doors leading onto the patio, and as soon as he spotted what he was looking for, he made a beeline for it.

Ox and Kate hurried with the puppy romping behind Bayou, wanting to see what he was going after. They reached the French doors simultaneously, yet they hung back, attempting to wedge themselves behind one of the doors.

Matt and Ali were facing each other, wine glasses in hand, and not aware of the world outside of their bubble.

As Bayou approached the imaginary love bubble, he dove forward, planting his nose into Matt's lap.

The puppy decided he wanted to investigate as well, but being much shorter than Bayou, he leaped and extended his bear-sized paws up and onto the swing.

With the weight of Bayou's body pushing forward and the puppy's, the swing tilted backward.

Since Matt and Ali had their hands full, their only option was to brace themselves with each other. The sudden movements sent waves of wine over the edge of their glasses.

Unsure of the motion under his paws, the puppy jumped off, and Bayou shuffled backward as the swing lurched forward.

Ali and Matt were wrapped around each other as though about to go overboard.

Bayou, concerned, let out a bark at the puppy. The startled pup scampered, tripped on his paws, and tumbled over onto his side.

Kate gasped as Ox reached for her and covered her mouth with his hand. "Shhh, he's okay."

He moved his hand on his wife's shoulder and squeezed it before wrapping his arms around her and pulling her close, kissing the top of her head.

Bayou walked over to the puppy and hovered over him as the chocolate fur ball sat up and rubbed the top of his head under his big brother's neck. The pup's eyes rolled up and back as if to be utterly delighted with the recognition. A moment of calm and acceptance washed over the area, and Ox could instantly tell that Bayou would be a great big brother.

On the other hand, Matt and Ali didn't look pleased about the current situation. Ali struggled to stand as wine ran down her arm.

Setting one foot on the ground, Matt held out his hand for Ali to use as leverage.

The liquid continued to run further down Ali's arm as she clutched her wine glass.

"I don't think I spilled any on my shirt." Ali craned her neck to examine it. "But it's chardonnay, so it shouldn't stain."

Matt reached out his hand. "You got a little right there." He put his finger on the shirt's collar near her neck.

Ox and Kate remained out of sight but could still see the action.

"His hand is still on her shirt," Ox whispered.

"They're going to kiss," Kate whispered.

"No, it's too soon," Ox retorted.

"Not when you're falling in love."

"They can't be; it's only been a few days." Ox shifted to get a better view.

The puppy yapped at Ali, and Bayou leaned back into his playful zoomies position. Matt's hand fell next to his side, and the moment was broken up by the two dogs that had pushed them together only a few seconds ago.

The dogs tore back through the French doors, past Ox and Kate, who hurried to the couch and flopped down.

With defeat across his brow, Matt entered, followed by Ali, who appeared just as unpleased.

"Is everything alright?" Ox watched the dogs chase each other through the living room.

Drawing his hand through his hair and down his neck, Matt futzed with his studded earring. Ali glanced at her empty wineglass and gave it a wave.

"Small interruption," Matt noted.

"Can I get you both more wine?" Kate offered, coming to her feet. "I'm sorry about the dogs." She hurried to the kitchen before they could respond.

Ox understood the awkwardness of losing the moment and didn't know what to say. He was not the best at these things. Remembering his parents' advice — fun facts were a perfect way to override any uncomfortable situation.

"Did you know you can make everything a song?" Ox forced a smile. "We could try it." Then he sang out, "we can try it and see how everything is a song."

Silence filled the room for a few seconds after he stopped, their faces frozen with shock.

Kate reappeared with an open bottle of cabernet.

"You and Kate are perfect for each other." Ali focused on Matt but managed to grab the bottle without making eye contact with Kate. "Would you like to take our wine to a dog-free area?"

"Yes, please." Matt bowed his head as though Ali was royalty.

Ox watched as Ali carried her glass and the bottle to the front door. Matt followed with a renewed spring in his steps.

The dogs whipped around the couch. Bayou's back end slammed into it, seeming to vibrate the entire room.

"We need a name for him," Kate said, placing a hand on her forehead. "We can't discipline him without one."

Chapter 37

Kate ran her finger under her eye, wiping the dampness away. "I've spent far too much time crying today, let alone this month."

Blowing her nose and crossing her legs, she readjusted the puppy in her lap. His tongue poked out, and a soft snore vibrated his lips. Beyond the windows, a crisp view of the moon illuminated the darkness.

"The puppy was supposed to . . . " Ox sat at the other end of the couch in their master bedroom. "I know you said you wanted a sibling for Bayou, but we can't have children. We need to discuss a di —"

Kate giggled a sigh. "That's why you were acting like I was asking for the world." She shook her head. "I meant a dog sibling, not a human sibling."

"*That* clarification would have been a lot more helpful." Ox pressed his palms on his legs. "You had me confused."

"Wait." Her heart rate increased. "Were you about to . . . " *He can't be wanting...*

Running her fingers over the puppy's chocolate fur, she took a deep breath. "I'm scared, Ox. What's going on?"

Nausea turned in her stomach at the silence stretched between them, and she started to shake.

He pressed his eyes shut. "I'm not enough for you. Losing you . . . losing you would be far more difficult than whatever the MS continues to do. But, it's time to face the truth. Us, we. We can't be tog —"

"Babe." She couldn't breathe with the crushing weight on her heart. "No, no. We will not get . . . that's what you were going to say the other night. That's why you've been acting differently." Kate couldn't even make the words come out.

When he opened his eyes, his lips parted. "I'm so grateful for your love every day. And I know, as I did that January, that you deserve someone who can give you the world. And it's not me. It has never been me."

"Ox, stop. I do deserve a man who gives me the world, and that man is you." Kate reached for him over the puppy, grabbing at Ox's shirt and pulling him forward. "If you ever have another thought about the D-word, please talk to me. Please don't allow it to fester inside of you. The D-word will never happen."

"Dessert?"

She pushed her words through the lump in her throat. "Always with a joke."

"Kate, you want a baby." The wrinkle between Ox's eyes creased.

She knew it was a statement of doubt and worry. "I have this fear of not being a mother. I want to have a baby because . . . I feel out of place without one. As a woman, everywhere I look, I see babies, children, and their mothers. It's like when you think about buying a car, and you can't decide, and from that moment on, suddenly you see *that* car everywhere you go, as though it's all anyone drives."

Kate felt as though she was about to choke on her emotions. "So, no — yes — no. I want to know what we could make together. That's something I'll always wonder about, even if I know we're not going to have children. I can't seem to shut my mind off about it, and I worry the thoughts will never go away."

"Please don't think I don't feel the same." He pressed his palm on her knee. "I want kids, but we know my MS would prevent me from being the father I want to be. The father a child deserves. We discussed this — the consequences. Not to mention, between my MS and your clumsiness, our kids would be caring for us far too soon."

A half-smile flickered on Kate's lips as she shifted and wrapped her free hand around her stomach. The puppy must've been dreaming as his paws twitched and spasmed. "I'm worried I'll never stop second-guessing the decision."

"Imagine being a parent right now. I can't. I'm tired at the end of the day without kids. I don't know how parents do it all." Ox made a fist and rested his wrist on top of his head. "Plus the cost of raising a child on top of my medical bills, especially if the child takes after you. Can you imagine the ER visits? It would be like Tim The Tool Man Taylor."

"Oh, gosh." Kate winced at the thought.

She knew all too well about the financial toll MS took on them, but she never thought their marriage might end over not having babies and was grateful Ox didn't go any further with his decision.

"So, no D. Promise me, Ox. Promise you understand that's not what I want and know it's not what's best for us." Kate's chin quivered.

He breathed deep as his chest expanded against his shirt. "I promise. And I want as much time to live life with you as possible." Ox squeezed her knee. "Maybe we can take up something that we participate in together, like boating."

"I'd love that. I want the Ox I first fell in love with back. My grab life by the ox horns, Ox."

"I want that too, and I'll make it happen. I just need some more time to work through losing my pilot's license." Ox glanced out the window.

Kate looked down at the furball asleep in her lap. "I understand." She sucked in a deep breath.

A crash in the distance startled them, waking Bayou but not the puppy.

Ox stood up, and Kate slid the dog off her lap and onto the couch. The Lab stretched and drifted back to sleep.

He opened the door but blocked Bayou from escaping. Kate slipped out and made their way into the hall with a view of the kitchen.

Matt was standing at the stove, and Ali was leaning on the island directly behind him.

"Are they cooking?" Ox asked.

"I think so." Kate tip-toed a few steps and made herself thin against the wall on the left.

She knew that seeing down the hall was hard with the kitchen lights on if someone wasn't standing in just the right spot.

Steam rose from a pot on the stove, and Matt moved it to the sink to pour it out. Ali had something shiny in her hand and tore the top off it. Matt set the pot back on the stove, and Ali squeezed out the packet over the top.

Kate's stomach moaned, realizing they were making boxed macaroni and cheese. She couldn't remember the last time she had the fake cheesy goodness.

Kate pondered where it came from since they didn't keep any in the inn. Ox made terrific mac and cheese, but there was something reminiscent of childhood and comforting about the box from the cupboard.

The kitchen's overhead lights reflected off a container with a clear top on the island's corner.

"They got chocolate cake," Kate mouthed.

"Don't worry, it's probably dark chocolate," Ox whispered. "They couldn't have driven since they were both drinking."

"There was that new grocery service; they must've had it delivered."

Matt served up two bowls at the island and stood opposite Ali as they leaned over and ate. Their wine glasses were nearly empty. Then Ali laughed at something and reached her hand out, touching Matt's chin. He paused, took a hold of her fingers, and then brought them to his lips and kissed the top of her hand.

Just watching the romance unfold made Kate's heart flutter.

Ali's body inched closer to Matt, and she paused when the light no longer showed between them.

Kate held her breath and her eyes widened. She reached for Ox's hand and squeezed it as though to contain her excitement from escaping.

Time seemed to freeze, the way Ali and Matt stared at each other in silence. They were clearly hitting it off, but there were many unknowns, one being Ali's unemployment. But when it came to love, Kate always believed they could work those things out if they were truly important, as she and Ox had done.

Ox placed his hands on Kate's shoulders and lowered his chin level with hers.

Matt's face drew even closer to Ali's and paused.

"Kiss her," Kate whispered.

But Matt didn't move; his hands were glued to his sides.

Kate pressed her palm to her forehead. *What's he doing? Kiss her!*

"What's he waiting for?" Ox's voice tickled her ear.

Then Ali's hands wrapped around Matt, and she yanked him forward, placing her lips on his. Matt's arms flung outwards from the motion but quickly found their way to the small of Ali's back.

Kate clenched her fists in the air and beamed a smile back at Ox.

Chapter 38

A wet nose crept up into his armpit, waking Ox. As he popped one eye open, he spotted the puppy's face. When Ox opened both eyes, the pup wiggled free and licked Ox's eye.

"Oh, I don't need more lubricant in there." Ox sat up, pushing off his elbows. "My eye is already wet enough."

Kate rolled over. "What's happening?"

He looked at the clock on the nightstand. "It's four in the morning. I guess the pup needs something."

Bayou's eyes fluttered open and closed, letting out a sigh as he remained curled up in the crook of Kate's legs.

"He still needs a name," Kate mumbled.

The mattress fluctuated under the weight as the puppy paced between him and Kate.

Ox scooped up the furball and rolled out of bed. "How about River? Bayou and River has a nice theme to it."

Kate turned her head; her curls displayed like a rising sun's rays on the pillow. "Okay, but we're not naming the next dog Ocean."

"Never say never." He wagged his finger and kissed her forehead.

A grateful feeling coursed through him like a sugar rush. He and Kate were back on track and nowhere near the derailment he assumed would've happened.

"Come, River, let's see what you need so early in the morning." Ox and River made their way out of the bedroom and down the hall.

Once outside, River sniffed around the plants and did his morning routine of sniff, potty, sniff, potty. Then he located a ball, nearly as big as his head, and clutched it in his jaw.

"River, it's too early for fetch. The sun is not even up yet. After we sleep a little more, we can play." Ox went to guide him back to the door, but River dodged his grasp.

River proceeded to gallop around the front yard with the ball clenched in his mouth. Ox hurried after him, finally able to snatch him up. Yet when Ox attempted to remove the ball from the clutches of River's teeth, he was unsuccessful.

"Release." Ox tugged at the ball. "Re-lease. River, release."

River aggressively shook his head without letting go of the ball, and Ox's grip slipped from it. The puppy and ball were one.

Ox made his way back inside the inn as River trotted behind him.

"I'm going back to bed," he whispered and rubbed his left eye.

With the ball still in his mouth, River followed him down the hall and into the bedroom. Ox lifted him back onto the bed and crawled under the covers.

He watched the puppy. "Lay down."

But River didn't want to do that. Instead, he wobbled over to Bayou and dropped the ball on his head. It rolled down and onto the floor.

River peered over the edge, unsure of his paws. With a final glance at the ball, he leaped off the bed equally with all four paws and landed on the floor with a thump.

Ox watched River, holding the ball in his mouth, come around the bed, and stood next to the nightstand. His chin barely reached the top of the mattress as he released the ball.

When Ox ignored him, River whimpered.

"No," Ox whispered and pushed the ball off the bed. "It's time for bed."

River let out a weak bark that startled himself as much as it did everyone else in bed.

Kate sat straight up, and Bayou's head lifted. "Why is he barking?"

"He's obsessed with that ball. I'll go play with him, but then we need to put the ball up." Ox threw back the covers as River slipped the ball into his mouth.

Together they headed back into the coolness of the summer morning. After about five minutes of fetch, Ox set the ball out of reach of River.

Confused, the puppy inspected the area, searching for the ball. Ox patted his leg. "Come, River, come."

Reluctant but not wanting to be left alone, River followed him back inside. Ox helped the pup onto the bed and covered himself up under the sheets.

"Okay, now go to sleep, River." Ox scrunched his face into the sternest look he could muster and then closed his eyes.

The bed shifted under the weight of the puppy's steps, and Ox popped an eye open to see if River was lying down next to Bayou.

Instead, River had grabbed his stuffed moose by the ear and dragged it toward Ox. Then the pup dropped the toy on Ox's cheek and stared at it just like he had the ball.

"For goodness sakes, River, it's time to sleep. No fetch." Ox picked up the moose and set it on the nightstand.

Ox rolled over and shut his eyes. Trying to ignore River was a much more challenging task than expected.

The puppy's paws pressed against Ox's body, followed by his stomach and then his back paws as River climbed over Ox. The pup climbed back over, and something dragged across Ox's shoulder.

He eased his eyes open and saw the stuffed moose hanging from River's mouth.

Ox shut his eyes and pretended to sleep. Maybe River would give up and go back to sleep if he thought no one was awake to play.

The mattress shifted, and a soggy moose landed on his head.

"River!" Ox moaned.

Kate rolled over. "What's going on?"

"I took the ball away, but I guess now he wants me to throw the moose."

"Well, throw the moose." Kate's hand blindly patted Ox. "The job of a daddy never ends."

"What about the job of a mommy?" He scratched at his morning hair.

"Shhhh, I'm only Bayou's mommy until the sun comes up."

Ox grumbled and picked up the moose and chucked it across the room.

Again, River four-pawed jumped off the bed, chased after the moose, and brought it back to Ox's side. With each throw, the scamper of puppy feet echoed in the silence of the morning.

After another three minutes of fetch, soreness crept up Ox's arm. "Okay, this is the last one, then it's time to sleep."

The moose went flying towards the bedroom window, and River returned with it in his mouth. As Ox hoisted the puppy into bed, he ran his hand over the soft chocolate fur. "Night, River."

A soggy moose and a panting puppy curled up between Ox and Kate. Drifting back to sleep, Ox set his hand on River's side just as the morning alarm beeped.

Chapter 39

During breakfast, Ali was missing from the table. A tall paper cup with a lid and Matt's name scribbled on it sat in front of him, letting her know he'd been up early.

Kate figured Ali was sleeping in after her and Matt's late night. The one thing the two of them didn't have in common, mornings. Ali and mornings didn't mix, unlike coffee and creamer.

Kate's cell phone vibrated in her pocket, and she pulled it out to read the alert.

Ali: MOUSE!

Back in college, Kate and Ali had used the code system to communicate important matters quickly or amid company. They didn't want to go with something anyone could figure out like the rather obvious: CODE RED. Instead, they picked three animals: Mouse, wolf, and bear. MOUSE meant something was up that needed discussing as soon as possible. WOLF was more of a mid-level threat, such as a date gone wrong and needed help to get out of it. BEAR meant immediate danger.

Matt and Ox were thumbs deep in whipped cream-covered crepes wrapped around a medley of berries, so Kate slipped her phone back into her pocket and excused herself from the table.

"He brought me a coffee," Ali stated and presented Kate with a paper cup that matched Matt's.

Kate entered the room and shut the door. "And?"

Upon closer examination, the words: GOOD MORNING were scribbled under her name.

"You!" Ali's eyes widened, and she gasped. "You're a little booger. This was a setup. This whole time!"

Kate sighed and tugged at Ali's pajamas as she lowered herself onto the floor at the side of the bed. "I have no idea what you're referring to."

"Kate Wil—Swanson," she corrected herself. "Matt and I."

"Yes." Kate leaned forward. "Did you want to go carve M&A into a tree with a heart?"

Ali picked up a pillow by the corner and swung it at Kate. "You set it up so Matt and I would be here at the same time."

"I didn't invent the calendar, but I could sing the "Calendar Girl" song," Kate started to sing and snapped her fingers.

"I can't believe you." Ali crossed her arms.

"Back to this." Kate pointed. "It seems a gentleman brings coffee for a woman he kissed last night." She pressed her palms into the bed as she leaned back and crossed her feet.

"You saw us?" Ali paused and sipped from the cup.

"Of course, you two were making a racket in the kitchen. I had to see what was up. You could've at least saved me a bowl."

"What do I do?" Ali waved her left hand in the air.

"About?"

"About falling for Matt."

"That's a good thing. How many romantic love connections did you have overseas? None, because you worked, and then you saw the sights and worked some more. It's time to unwind, finally. Be in love."

"Love can lead to marriage, and marriage leads to babies." Ali picked at the lid on the paper cup.

Kate sat up straight.

"I'm sorry. I shouldn't have said it like that. I know . . . " Ali's voice trailed off.

A thud vibrated against the bedroom door. Followed by another as the door burst open, and Bayou trotted in like he got wind of a party he hadn't been invited to but should've.

"Oh, I meant to tell you, the door doesn't latch," Ali stated.

Bayou flopped down at the edge of the rug, just shy of Kate's bare feet.

"I'll let Ox know." She lowered herself onto the floor and petted Bayou the length of his body as his eyes scanned the room. "Now tell me about last night."

"It was . . . it was like the movies. A romantic movie where they end with a kiss. A slow-burning romance. When I'm around Matt, I feel nervous, like I'm on stage giving a presentation. But I *want* to give this presentation."

"I never got around to asking you how it went at Fort Wayne after I snuck off to take photos?" Kate rested her back on the side of the mattress and cocked her head up at Ali.

"Matt was a gentleman, and you would've thought those bunkers were still in use. The way he guided me through them with caution."

"That's so sweet. Have you and Matt talked about dating?"

"He lives in New York."

"You've always wanted to live in New York." Kate smiled. "And I wouldn't have to fly over the ocean to see you."

"You don't have to fly at all if I stay in Washington." Ali ran her finger around the lid of the coffee cup.

"New York bagels and cheesecake." Kate's eyes glazed over, and she licked her lips. "Pizza."

"But none of the places I submitted my resume to are in New York. I've had a few virtual interviews from the ones I sent out, but no responses yet." Ali shook her head. "What am I talking about? I'm acting like Matt, and I are moving in together or something. We haven't even known each other for a week."

"Need I remind you again about Ox and me."

Ali tilted her head. "But you and Ox are . . . you and Ox. No one can be as cute and as perfect."

Kate placed her hand on her heart. "Aww."

"It's true."

"What's to say that you can't have the same perfect love?"

"Life, reality."

"There's only one way to find out if there's something special between you two." Kate brought herself to her knees. "You need to spend every second with each other before Matt leaves."

Chapter 40

Matt reached for a small bowl of homemade whipped cream. "I kissed her last night."

Ox looked in the direction of the inn's stairs. "I know."

"You know?" Matt's forehead creased.

"I saw you two, and technically Ali kissed you."

"Oh." Matt cut the crepe with his fork and stacked them like blocks until he couldn't fit any more pieces on it. "Ali is beautiful. I've never met anyone like her before. She seems so out of my league."

"How so?"

Matt set his fork down and picked up his paper cup. "This is going to sound harsh, but she's smart."

"You've been exclusively dating . . . women with low IQs?"

Matt shook his head. "No, not on purpose. I mean, the women I date are smart, but Ali is a different level of intelligence. She's driven, unapologetic, and put together. I've been in relationships with women who are at the beginning of their life's puzzle. Their pieces are lost, upside down, and don't fit where they thought they would. Not Ali, she's that feeling when you stick the last piece in, and it's complete."

"Ali's a completed puzzle?" Ox inhaled a piece of crepe with strawberry slices and whipped cream into his mouth.

"Ali's a 3D puzzle." Matt smiled.

Ox swallowed. "You have a *real* way of describing a woman."

"Thanks, man." Matt picked his fork back up.

Ox snickered to himself; maybe later, when he and Kate were cozy in bed with the dogs, he could compare her to Jenga.

"What should I do?" Matt asked.

Ox felt River stretch out at his feet, and his puppy belly lapped over his toes. "About Ali?"

"I'm in New York. She's not."

Before Ox could respond, Bayou trampled down the steps with Ali and Kate behind him. River sprang to life, weaving out from under the table.

"After breakfast, I thought we could head over to Hopewood Island. There's a ferry that leaves every thirty minutes." Kate refreshed her cup of coffee from the carafe and sat in the chair closest to Ox.

"That sounds enjoyable." Ali sat in a chair that Matt had pulled out for her at the kitchen table.

"I'd love to go, but Bayou and I have another therapy appointment for a chemo patient." Ox picked up his mug.

"Then let's wait." Kate rubbed Ox's back with her free hand. "We don't want you missing out on another adventure."

"That's silly. There's no reason to sit around here for half the day, especially with the sun out. Rain is in the forecast for tomorrow." Ox looked at his watch. "Besides, someone needs to be with River. He can't be locked up in his crate for too long."

Kate frowned. "You're right. Matt and Ali should go. I can stay here with River."

"Parental sacrifices." Ox winked.

A smile warmed his wife's face.

"I'm game if Ali is also?" Matt's vision went to Ali.

"Absolutely." Ali opened the cloth napkin and laid it in her lap.

Kate used her finger to scoop a dollop of whipped cream off Ox's crepe. "Just so you know, babe. Since River is three months old, he's technically not a puppy."

"She's right, Ox. Kate wanted a puppy. But be careful, or this place will look like the set of *101 Dalmatians* with all those dogs running around." Ali snickered.

Ox choked on his crepe and patted his chest to try and help clear it. That's precisely what he was afraid of, his wife's puppy fever.

Chapter 41

"You might be handsome, River, but you're sure a fetch menace." Kate shook the stuffed moose he dragged outside at him. "Come on, let's go potty."

She patted her leg as River followed her down the steps into the front yard.

Immediately River spotted his ball and snatched it up into his mouth, leaving the soggy moose in the grass.

"No," she warned. "We played ten games of fetch already and went for a walk. It's time to potty and then take a nap."

Refusing to drop the ball, River paced the front yard and then approached her and looked up.

She shook her head. "No, River."

The puppy fell into a sloppy-sit. The ball in his mouth pulled his lips up and to the sides, making it look like he was deviously smiling at her. She crossed her arms.

Suddenly, River sprung up, hurried off, dropped his ball, and Kate realized what was about to happen. And it was over before it even began.

She covered her face with her hands. "River, you pooped on your ball."

The puppy turned around and stared at the ball. He wanted to get it, the way he leaned over it, trying to find out how to go about saving it from the stinky situation. His paw lifted in the air but hovered before he backed up, realizing he needed help.

Kate tucked her unruly curls behind her ears. "I guess that's one way to get you to stop bugging for fetch."

River barked and barked again, staring the ball down.

"I guess not. River, shhh, hang on. Thank goodness we can clean and sanitize it."

Kate walked over to the garage and grabbed two plastic bags.

When she returned to the scene of the crime, River hadn't moved an inch. He continued to stare at the poop-covered ball, and she did her best to handle the gross situation.

"Please don't ever do this again." Kate hosed off the ball, sprayed hydrogen peroxide on it, and then sprayed it off again.

"If you insist on pooping *with* your ball, at least hang onto it."

As she handed River's ball back, Ox's truck rumbled up the driveway. Now she truly understood how a parent felt when another adult comes home just in time to help disperse some of the load.

Bayou dashed out from the garage with Ox behind him.

"Did you have a good therapy session?" she asked the dog as she squatted down and buried her face into his soft fur.

"He did great, as usual. On the other hand, I was not." Ox approached the edge of the front lawn. "I'm not sure I'll ever get used to it."

When Kate stood up, he draped his arm over her shoulder as they watched River alert to Bayou's return. Then, with zoomies in full effect, they chased each other around the front yard.

"I know it's been an adjustment." She wrapped her arm around her husband's waist.

"I already miss flying, and I hate the hospital."

"Why don't we go on vacation?" Her hand rubbed the middle of his back.

"With a new puppy?"

Kate watched as Bayou rolled over and River climbed over him.

She pouted. "I guess having kids does prevent parents from doing things."

"Are you always going to talk about our dogs like they're kids?" Ox kissed the top of her head.

"Are you going to have a problem with that?"

"No, I just wanted to make sure I was on the same page as you this time." Ox wrapped her in his embrace. Taking his fingers, he ran them over her cheek.

Kate stood on her tippy toes and leaned her head up as Ox brought his lips to hers. There were still times when he kissed her, causing dizziness to wash over her body. She felt the world tilt, and she wrapped her arms tighter around him to keep from falling.

Something dropped at her foot, and they pulled from their kiss. Kate took a step back to find the shiny ball and River.

"He looks like he's smiling." Ox rested his hand on his wife's hip.

"He does. River's a happy dog, but I can see how quickly he could wear someone out."

"Good thing he has us then because we're not ones to give up."

She rested her head on his chest. "Oh." Kate grabbed her phone from her pocket and opened up her social media app.

"Speaking of not giving up. Look at what Ali posted." She handed the phone to Ox.

In the photo, Matt's arm was draped over Ali's shoulder. It was noticeable he was the one holding the camera to get them and the Puget Sound in the shot. They were on the upper deck of the ferry boat to Hopewood Island.

She sighed at the thought. "Do you see the caption? It's just hearts. Two red hearts."

"And you've psychoanalyzed the hearts to mean?" Ox handed Kate her phone back.

"That she doesn't know what to call or label their friendship or relationship or whatever is blooming between them."

"She's posted two other photos. They're eating lunch at the restaurant that's right off the ferry terminal."

"Oh, the one we never remember the name of?" Ox mentioned.

Kate scrolled down to it on the phone and showed him. Ox was the only one she knew who didn't have any social media accounts outside of her dad.

Her phone dinged.

"Oh, that means she posted a new one." Kate scrolled back up to the top. "They look so cozy."

In the newest picture, Ali rested her head on Matt's shoulder, and he rested his cheek on the top of her head.

She slid the phone back into her pocket. "I hope we can help them see they need to pursue a relationship beyond this week."

"If it's meant to be, like it was with us, it'll happen." He took a hold of her hand. "Do you know what I was thinking would be perfect right now?"

"What?" She bent down and picked up the ball, tossing it across the yard for River.

"A *Magnum P.I.* marathon. Or at least as many episodes as we can watch before they return." He squeezed her hand. "I miss cuddling with you, and it seems as though it's been a million years since we last did."

River dropped the retrieved ball at her feet. "We might have to clear that with the fetch master two-thousand."

"We could try ignoring him." He prevented Kate from picking up the ball by holding her upright.

River tilted his head, looked at the ball and then his parents, then the ball again.

Kate and Ox crossed their arms and shook their heads no.

The puppy picked up the ball and dropped it. And when that did nothing, he did it again.

"No," Ox stated.

River let out a bark and backed up, keeping his eyes on the ball.

"I think we're going to lose this battle." Kate bit the side of her cheek.

"And I'm okay with that." Ox picked up the ball and chucked it.

Chapter 42

"I knew it was too good to be true," Matt groaned.

Ox and Matt sat on the back patio, watching the last of the sun's rays say goodbye as they faded into a glow of purple and blue.

Matt crossed his arms over his chest. "Deep down, I could tell it was going to end up like this. Like a bad casserole lingering in your gut."

"What happened?" Ox asked.

Throughout dinner, Matt and Ali hadn't said a word, let alone allowed their eyes to meet. The only noises between the two were sounds of utensils scraping across the plates.

"Everything was going great. We had a nice lunch and walked around Hopewood Island, holding hands. But on the ferry ride back, I asked if we could see where this relationship might go, and she said something about not knowing where she's living or what her future holds, so she didn't want to commit to anything." Matt rotated his bottle of beer on the armrest of the chair. "I explained we could figure it all out. Figure out the distance between our living situations. But if we didn't even give it a try, we would never know."

In response, Ox cracked his knuckles.

"Who falls for a woman, and before he can finish falling, he's already rejected. This guy." Matt shoved a thumb into his chest and swigged from the bottle. "I mean, is there something I can say or do to make her change her mind?"

Ox swatted at a mosquito.

"Talking didn't get me anywhere. What else can I possibly do?"

Ox squeezed his hand into a fist, his muscles ached. "Show her."

The cell phone in Ox's pocket vibrated. "Excuse me one second, Matt." He fished it out between his fingers and answered the call. "Hello?"

"Yes, I'm calling about the Cessna for sale?"

Ox blinked, taken aback by hearing the words. Even though he'd put an ad in for the plane, it didn't mean he found the entire situation easy to swallow.

"Yes, when do you have time to swing by? It's at the Crooked River Airport." Ox wrapped his palm around the bottle, the dampness of the label cool on his skin.

"How about Saturday at noon? By the way, I'm Paul."

"Nice to speak with you Paul, I'm Ox. Saturday at noon works for me. I'll meet you at the entrance for the private hangars."

"Great, see you Saturday."

The line clicked off on Paul's end.

"Bye," Ox mumbled, snapping his phone closed.

"So, you're selling your plane?"

Ox flicked the phone as it spun between his middle finger and thumb like a wheel. After slipping it into his pocket, Ox pressed his back into the Adirondack chair.

Matt cleared his throat. "Don't want to talk about the plane I take it?"

A breeze kicked through the branches of the nearby trees, bringing with it the scent of evergreen and bark.

"Nothing to say." Ox put the bottle to his lips and took a swig. "Dogs aren't cheap, things are breaking around the inn, and my MS is not getting better. I can hold onto the past or accept the future. But I can't do both."

Matt nodded and stared off into the woods. "Change is life, and life is change."

"Sorry, what were we saying before the phone call?"

Stretching out his legs, Matt stomped the heels of his loafers into the decking. "Something about showing her, showing Ali. But, man, I have no idea how I can show her."

"I was thinking about Bayou working with chemotherapy patients and how their doctors and even loved ones can tell them everything will be alright, but that's not enough. What works is the action." Ox glanced outwards, noticing the sky's colors shifting further into the darkness of the night. "The action of showing. Bayou will take his paw and place it on the person. Rest his chin on their lap. Bayou's actions calm the client, showing them that he's there even with the anxiety and loss of hope. He gives them something concrete, tangible."

Matt nodded his head and sat forward in the chair. "It makes sense. I just need to figure out what I have to offer someone of her caliber. And soon, I'm leaving in two days."

Chapter 43

"Bear," Ali mumbled into the pillow, holding her cell phone in the air.

Kate allowed River and Bayou to come inside and then shut the door. Her best friend had her suitcase open on the bed. Kate folded her leg under her thigh as she sat down.

River's paws stretched up onto the side of the bed, and Kate lifted him like a toddler from a crib.

"I think I messed everything up." Ali's hand went to her necklace.

"Stop packing and tell me what happened? You both were so quiet during dinner. It was a bit awkward."

"When we were out to lunch, Matt wanted to approach the subject of a relationship. It's too soon, and I don't — no — I won't do long distance."

River wiggled around in Kate's lap until he found a comfortable spot. His head rested in her outreached hand while Bayou took claim of the rug and stretched himself out.

"Okay, so I can understand the argument against a long-distance relationship, but why is a relationship too soon?" Kate observed River's chest rise and fall with each breath. "And why does it have to be long-distance? You're jobless, which means you don't have to remain at a distance."

"No one falls in love — like that." Ali snapped her fingers. "I mean besides you and Ox. It's the stuff of movies. Unrealistic movies and unrealistic romance novels. If televisions weren't so expensive, I'd slingshot a hardcover romance novel into a romance movie and knock the couple upside the head."

"Well, that's a violent image." Kate pressed her hand into her collarbone. "Are you calling Ox and I unrealistic? You don't think the writers base those movies on something in real life?"

"You and Ox are one in a million." Ali picked up her glass of merlot leftover from dinner and sipped it. "Writers create those romances out of their dreams and fantasies, not from real life."

"When will you stop running away from everything you don't have the answer to."

"I'm not running." Ali held up a boot in each hand. "I'm checking out a day early and heading to the Airbnb I rented."

"That's running."

Ali tossed a shirt into the suitcase and threw her hands out in front of her. "What am I supposed to do? I must have a plan, order to my life. Everything about Matt is not in order. It's not planned. It's unknown."

Kate looked around the room. "Where's your notebook? You need *the* list."

"The list?" Ali huffed. She removed a black and pink striped notebook from her suitcase's hidden pocket and tossed it near Kate, missing River. "Here, you use it for your life. A list is for things you want to figure out. There is nothing to figure out about Matt and me."

River continued to sleep as the bed dipped when Ali returned, and Kate held her hand out, wiggling her fingers. Ali pouted and reached for a pen, slapping it in Kate's hand.

Kate drew a line down the middle of the page and labeled the two columns GOOD and BAD.

"Perfect match." Kate batted her eyes.

Ali crossed her arms. "That could go in either one."

"Don't be like that." Kate pointed with her free hand and added it to the GOOD column.

"I have no idea where I'll be living."

"And it provides you with the opportunity to do whatever you want. Nothing is holding you back from exploring this relationship."

"But I also have no way to support myself."

Kate pressed her lips together. "You haven't heard back from any of your virtual interviews yet?"

"To be honest, I haven't checked." Ali reached for her phone on the nightstand. "Except for taking photos, I've been ignoring my notifications."

Kate looked down at River, who was now softly snoring. His body pressed against the suitcase, and his chin rested on her knee.

"Let me check my voicemail." Ali held her phone to her ear, listening as she played something, the muffled voice came through, but Kate couldn't make out anything that was said.

Ali lowered the cell phone, and her mouth hung open. "I was offered a position . . . in Australia."

"That's nowhere near New York."

Chapter 44

"What do you mean a job offer in Australia?" Ox whispered to Kate, hovering over the kitchen's island.

"She's going to take it. It gives her a clear-cut path and plan." Kate refilled her wine glass. "She canceled her reservation at the Airbnb and booked a flight out tomorrow morning."

"Then Matt's big show of action will be exactly what Ali needs."

A clunk near the top of the stairs drew their attention. Ali appeared and carried her suitcase down the steps. "I'm leaving some of my luggage here for tomorrow morning. One less thing to carry down."

The inn's warm nighttime glow cast shadows across the hardwood floors.

"What's going on?" Matt appeared from the living room and approached Ali. "You're leaving early? I thought you'd be here for another two days."

"A job has come up." Ali ran a hand over her necklace.

"That's great. Where? Perhaps New York?"

Ali shook her head. "No, it's in Australia."

"Australia? That's not even in America." Matt slumped over as though all the bones in his body had failed to support him. "What about us?"

Ali slid her hands into her front pockets and looked at her feet. "There's not an 'us.' There can't be an 'us.'"

"Well, I'd like there to be an us."

Ox stepped forward. "You'll be staying for the big breakfast Matt has planned, right?"

Matt's forehead creased. "Big breakfast?"

Ox gave him intense wide eyes.

"Yes, yes." Matt, catching on, pointed his finger. "The big breakfast — I'm making tomorrow. And you can't leave on an empty stomach. Flying rules state that, I think, in the laminated manual in the seatback. One must fly on a full stomach."

"That doesn't sound right," Kate mumbled.

Ox spun around and motioned for her to zip it. Smiling, she clenched her jaw and mouthed sorry.

"Ox, if I could speak with you for a minute, please." Matt headed into the kitchen. "Need to work out a few minor details for tomorrow."

"Yes, we do want it to be a surprise, as much as a breakfast can be, so maybe Kate and Ali would like to enjoy some wine on the back patio." Ox cleared his throat. "Ladies, stargaze for a while."

Kate grabbed the bottle and snatched her best friend by the arm, rushing her out of the kitchen.

"Minor detail," Matt hissed once the women were gone. "What big breakfast?"

"Did you have a better plan?"

"No." Matt rubbed his temples. "Wait, yes, a charcuterie board."

"For breakfast? You want to impress her with rolled-up meats and cheeses?"

Matt shoved his hands in his pockets. "Meats and cheeses can be impressive. You can cut the cheese into star shapes. I saw it on Instagram."

Ox rested his hand on his chin. "That's a great plan if Ali was a five-year-old and we were having a slumber party."

Matt grumbled. "You know I can't cook, right?"

"What do you mean, you're single. What do you eat for dinner?"

"I order in. It's New York City."

Ox turned to the refrigerator and flung both doors wide open. "I can help then."

"Thanks, but how is a big breakfast going to be a grand gesture?"

"We can make it romantic. Like in those movies, you know, Meg Ryan, Tom Hanks."

Matt flopped into the stool at the end of the island. "Is it too soon to propose?"

Ox looked over his shoulder. "Yes, this isn't a *Dateline* romance."

Matt rested his elbows on the island and scanned the kitchen. "I know she loves cinnamon rolls. Maybe we could make that with fresh fruit and bacon."

"I have an excellent cinnamon roll recipe, but it needs to rest overnight."

Matt waved his finger. "Yes, you made those when I was here last time." He stood up. "I'll get fresh flowers. She loves plumeria. But not a bouquet, I'll go all out. Make it look like a flower shop exploded."

"If the breakfast doesn't work, then maybe the allergies will keep her grounded." Ox removed the ingredients for the cinnamon rolls. "You've learned a lot about her favorites in a short time."

"When she talks, I listen." Matt chuckled. "I think this might be the first time."

Ox cocked his head.

"Don't get me wrong, I listen to women, but it usually goes in one ear and out the other. But not with Ali."

Ox pulled out the cookbook with the page folded down, marking the cinnamon roll recipe.

"Ox, I don't know how to make her understand that we have something. Something great between us. And now I have to compete against a continent. The big breakfast is a great idea, but I need something more, something to top off the breakfast. Before it was fighting the distance between states and now . . . they have kangaroos!"

"Help me with this." Ox removed a mixing bowl and set it to the side where he needed Matt to stand. "Someone needs to teach you how to bake."

"Thanks," Matt mumbled. "Doesn't she know they have a million dangerous bugs roaming the land?"

"I wouldn't move there. On the other hand, traveling there might be nice."

"What can I do that's bigger than Australia?" Matt punched his fist into the palm of his other hand. "That's it!"

Ox set the butter in a small bowl and put it in the microwave. "What?"

"If I can't get her anything bigger than Australia, then I'll give her Australia."

"Give her Australia?" Ox added milk and the yeast to the bowl. "You're not going to do some life-size paper-mâché of anything, are you?"

"Why would I? No, I'm going to Australia."

"As in visit?"

Matt's posture was proud. "No, as in moving there. If she's going to Australia, so will I."

"That's the craziest idea I've ever heard."

"Good, then it just might work."

Chapter 45

Late last night, when Ox came to bed, he'd mentioned Matt's big plan, but Kate was too sleepy to understand it fully. So, when she woke up in the morning, she thought it'd been a dream until the smell of cinnamon rolls hit her nose. Looking around the bedroom, she noticed Ox and the dogs were missing.

As she dressed for the day, she played over the events of the previous night. Kate insisted they return to Ali's room and finish the list, but her best friend had already made up her mind about the new job. There was zero room for discussion. Instead, she and Ali watched an unsolved murder documentary on her tablet, the exact opposite of a romantic movie, on purpose. It was like they were back in college and avoided anything that required them to face their real problems.

Kate hoped Matt's grand gesture was enough to give them a chance at seeing what the future might hold for them, together, wherever that might be.

Exiting the bedroom, she smiled at the smell of bacon and sweet sugar in the air. Then the scent of citrusy-peach hit her, traveling up her nose.

The kitchen had vases upon vases of pink and white plumerias. Ox was at the grill on the stove frying up the bacon while Matt stood opposite him cutting up a cantaloupe and strawberries.

Bayou was lying between the two men. River sat with his back pressed up against the back of Ox's legs, so if he tried to move, it would be impossible to ignore him.

As Kate entered the kitchen, she grabbed the attention of all four. "Good morning, everyone."

"Morning," chimed the men.

Footsteps came from behind, and Kate turned around to see Ali coming down the steps, carrying the last of her luggage. She had on smoky gray leggings, tan half-ankle boots, and a maroon top.

"Wow, the flowers . . . there must be a thousand here. They're beautiful." Ali stepped into the kitchen and clasped her hands together. "Oh, and it smells so yummy."

"Good morning, Ali." Matt stirred the bowl of cut fruit.

"Good morning." Ali pulled out a chair and sat down.

Matt set the bowl of fruit in front of her. "I picked up your favorite latte; let me know if I can reheat it for you."

"Thank you, that's very kind of you. And thank you for all these flowers. I wish I could take them with me."

Matt didn't reply as he took a seat next to Ali.

"The cinnamon rolls are ready." Ox lifted the serving dish of sticky icing-covered buns, carried it to the table, and wedged the dish between two vases of white plumerias.

Matt looked deeply at Ali as she used the tongs to separate a cinnamon roll from the bunch and set it on her plate; the icing ran down the sides.

Kate stared at them so intensely that Ox elbowed her as he walked by. She took the hint and sat opposite so she could keep watching Ali and Matt.

After Matt had piled his plate with all the essentials, Kate and Ox did the same. They remained fixed on their friends as though a season finale of a television show.

"This is amazing. Perfect for a rainy morning." Ali pressed her lips together.

Kate took bites of food without looking down at her plate.

Although Ali and Matt wouldn't appreciate the stare-down, they didn't notice it as neither looked anywhere but their plates. Matt fidgeted in his chair and bit his lower lip.

Bayou, unhappy with the current food-dropping situation, moved from Ali over to Ox in the hopes of achieving a better outcome. River decided to take his chances and remained at Matt's feet.

"River." Kate patted her leg. "Come here, no begging."

River didn't move.

She smacked her leg louder. "River, come here."

As soon as River moved, he paused. His eyes caught something. He leaned toward a piece of paper sticking out of Matt's pant pocket. The puppy's lips gave it a quick taste.

"River, no," Kate said. "Leave it."

But the puppy didn't listen.

The paper slid from Matt's pocket as River held it in his mouth and exited the kitchen in a fast wobble.

Kate's eyes widened, flashed a look of alert to Ox, and mouthed, "River has the ticket."

Ox tilted his head, allowing the words to sink in. As soon as Ox understood, they sprung from their chairs.

"River, give that back," Ox warned, standing at the edge of the living room step.

River was on his belly, his four legs outstretched as though he had no bones in his body.

The paper was hanging out both sides of his mouth as though the puppy didn't have any idea what he'd stolen, only that he wanted to savor it.

Kate got on her hands and knees and crawled over to River. "Give me that ticket."

"A ticket?" Ali's voice came from behind her. "What's going on?"

Kate lunged for the paper, grabbing the edge of it with one hand and her other hand around River's mouth, trying to pry it open. "Give it to me."

River wiggled backward, slipping out of Kate's grasp, and darted around the living room, looking for an escape route.

Matt, Ox, Ali, and Bayou were standing at the landing of the room. There was no way River would get past them.

Kate rose to her feet as River made a break for it between Ali and Bayou. Then the yellow lab moved, turning his body lengthwise just in time for River to smack head-first into his side.

The puppy stumbled, and the paper drifted to the floor like a wet leaf.

Ox and Ali reached for it at the same time, but Ali was quicker.

"What's this, and why is everyone so concerned over it?" Ali opened up the folded, soggy piece of paper.

Matt slid it from her grasp. "It's my ticket to Australia. I want to see where our relationship goes, and I'm willing to give up everything in New York to make it happen."

Ali's mouth fell open, and she placed her hand on her chest. "I'm sorry, but no. You can't. I can't."

"I'm giving up everything to join you." Matt pleaded. "Nothing in your life has to change."

Ali turned, hurried past her luggage, and out the front door, leaving it wide open.

The sound of rain came through the entry along with a gust of cold air. Bayou approached the door, looked left, and then chased after Kate's best friend.

In shock, it took a few seconds for Kate to realize what happened before she took after Ali, catching the last little bit of the yellow tail dipping behind a tree on the path leading around the backside of the inn.

Kate had thrown on flip-flops, the worst combination for a trail, especially in the rain. She followed the winding path speckled with overgrown branches.

"Ali," Kate called out. "Bayou." She stepped around the bend and spotted the yellow Lab.

"Bayou." She grew closer to find Ali with her back to her. Kate gave Bayou a rub on the head. "Great job, buddy."

The dog sniffed the ground as Kate put her hands on her best friend's shoulders and turned her around.

Ali had tears streaming down her cheeks, smudging the black eyeliner under her eyes.

Kate frowned. "Oh, Ali, why do you keep running? What's so wrong about seeing where a relationship with Matt will go?"

Ali sniffled and wiped her tears with the back of her hand. "Love doesn't happen like *this*. If I allow myself to settle down, I could get hurt. No, I *will* get hurt. I don't need to be in love."

"You may not need to be, but don't you want to be?" Kate allowed her hands to fall to her sides. "Don't you want to wake up and smile at the beautiful person next to you? To have someone by your side no matter what happens in life?"

"I don't want to lose who I am to be in love, to be married." Ali crossed her arms.

"Do you think a man could ever change you to the point that you'd lose yourself?"

"It doesn't matter. This wasn't the plan, Kate. Sure, I was supposed to come here for a vacation, but not because I lost my job. And I wasn't supposed to meet anyone, let alone fall in love." Ali's hand went to her mouth as her eyes watered.

"Stop acting like it's a bad thing. Falling in love is like the rainbow at the end of a storm. You don't expect it, but when you find it, it's beautiful, and you're grateful for it. I understand the suddenness of it makes you uncomfortable and unsure. But it doesn't mean you push it away and ignore it."

"It's just not in my plan."

"My goodness, Ali, falling in love is not something you plan." Kate pushed a strand of rain-dampened curls off her forehead. "I think making those lists all these years held you back. An excuse, instead of realizing what's right in front of you."

"I'm scared about what's right in front of me." Ali blinked.

"Then maybe it's time to take the biggest chance of your life."

Chapter 46

Ox followed Matt up the stairs to his room and blocked the door as Matt attempted to slam it shut.

"Calm down. You're acting like a teenager," Ox snapped.

"What am I supposed to do now?" Matt ran his hand through his hair. "Forget I'm in love with her?"

"You could go after her." Ox crossed his arms and leaned on the doorframe. Weakness coursed through his body.

"And say what? The same thing I've been saying? She doesn't want to listen, and if she does listen, she's already made her mind up. This is why I've always avoided anything serious with women."

Paws stomped up the steps and caused Ox to turn his head down the hall. River was heading his way, carrying a green rubber ball in his mouth.

"How'd you get the ball inside?" He petted River on the head as the ball fell from his mouth and landed on Ox's foot. "No, fetch. We need to help Matt."

"I don't need help. I need Ali." Matt paced the room. "No, I need to get *over* Ali."

"Go tell her that." Ox checked his watch. "Not the getting over her part, the part about needing her. Ali's flight doesn't leave for another six hours. And I can print out a new boarding pass for you. There's still a chance. Give Kate time to talk to her. If you hide away and don't try, you'll regret it."

Matt set his suitcase on the bed and unzipped it, flopping the lid open. "What if this is my life?"

"Packing?"

"Being alone." Matt lowered onto the edge of the bed, and River picked up the ball, went to him, dropping it at his feet.

"Have you tried thinking positively about your outcome with Ali?" Ox suggested.

Matt ignored River even though the puppy had picked up the ball three more times and dropped it in front of him. "Think positively? What's next, tarot cards?"

Ox gave a short laugh. "No, I'm serious. Maybe tarot cards work — I've never tried. Listen," Ox shifted his weight onto his other foot, "the one thing about Kate that drew me to her was her relentless ability to see the positive of being with me. Show Ali you're not giving up on her. Let her understand the positive aspect of moving forward with a relationship. Ali's scared. Show her you're her safety net."

River picked up his ball and played with it in his mouth, squeezing it as it made sucking noises.

"Just a second, buddy," Ox said.

"If only it were so easy. Hey, do you have one of those earpieces, like in the movies? You can feed me my lines. You're much better than I am."

"Sorry, this inn is not *that* full service. Romance is between the two people *in* the romance."

Ox felt his knees weaken and his face flushed. "I hate to ask . . ." he rubbed his forehead as embarrassment washed over him. "Would you mind helping me down the stairs? I need my cane."

Matt didn't say a word but walked toward him, wrapping his arm around Ox and guided him down the hall.

"I'm having flashbacks of the time Kate and I got turned around in the woods," Matt mentioned.

Ox hummed a chuckle as they took one step at a time to the first floor of the inn. When they reached the last step, Ox fought the weakness and numbness coursing through him.

"Where's your cane? I'll grab it for you." Matt made sure Ox was stable before he let go of his arm.

"In my office, near the desk."

Matt hurried off, and Ox turned, glancing up the stairs, wondering what happened to River.

The puppy was standing at the top step, and as soon as they made eye contact River let the ball drop. The ball bounced haphazardly down each step and then rolled to a stop at the bottom.

River lumbered down the stairs and had snatched the ball back into his mouth by the time Matt returned with Ox's cane.

"Thank you," Ox sighed.

Matt put his hand out and rested it on Ox's shoulder. "Are you alright if I go after Ali?"

Ox waved his hand and took a few steps with his cane. "Yes, River will keep me company."

He watched Matt open the front door, cross his fingers, and held them up in the air.

Chapter 47

"Ali?" Matt's voice echoed through the trees. "Ali?"

Kate spotted Matt through the rain heading their way. "Give him a chance. Give yourself a chance."

She tapped her leg, and Bayou walked alongside her, passing Matt. "Don't give up, she's as stubborn as Ox, but she's worth it," Kate reassured him.

Matt nodded. "Thanks."

Kate continued just around the tree and then put her hand up, motioning for Bayou to stop. The rain made it difficult to hear, but closing her eyes and focusing might help.

"I know this is sudden," Matt said. "I didn't come to the Inn of the Hoods to find anything other than a Playstation, but you . . . you, Ali, you're like the mint on a pillow at a fancy hotel."

Kate scrunched her face and covered her laughter. *I don't think I'm hearing all the words correctly.*

"You like me enough to move your entire life across the curled to another gum tree?" Ali asked. "Your job's in New York, and you love New York."

Kate stepped a few feet closer to hear better.

She saw Matt brush Ali's hair behind her ear with his hand. Ali took a hold of his fingers, pulling them to her cheek.

"Don't make me be *your* regret," Ali said. "I can't ask you to move to Australia. I'm not even sure how long I'll be living there. I might hate it and end up moving again."

Ali's hand fell from Matt's hand, but he left it on her cheek.

"And if we work out, then I guess I'll just have to follow you wherever you decide to go next."

Ali's hand moved to Matt's waist. "And what if this is just a fling, a lust of sorts? A summer camp romance?"

Matt's hand wrapped around the back of Ali's neck, and Kate found herself leaning forward to get a closer look.

"I've never felt this way about another woman in my life. I'm falling in love with you, Ali."

Ali glanced down for a second, and when she looked back up, she whispered something, but Kate couldn't hear what she said. Then in a blink, Ali and Matt were kissing. And not just any kiss, because Kate swore she saw Ali's legs buckle at the knees.

Kate clapped silently as the rain ran down her fingertips. "Come on, Bayou," she whispered, "our work here is done."

They headed back to the inn to find Ox sleeping on the couch in the living room. River had curled up next to him, his green ball tucked under his chin.

She noticed Ox's cane on the floor below, causing her smile to disappear. Kate watched them sleeping just a second longer and then looked at Bayou and gave her head a slight jerk to motion for him to come with her.

Bayou trotted behind her into the master bedroom. She changed out of her damp shirt and tried to locate a pair of shoes for the day.

"It would sure be nice if I could wear my Crocs." She held up one of them. "Any time you want to show me where you hid my other one, *that* would be great."

Bayou turned and exited the closet as though tip-toeing away.

"Kate?" Ox's voice called from the living room.

She headed down the hall, and just when she was about to step down into the room, the front door opened, and she turned, spotting Ali and Matt arm in arm walking in. Doing so caused Kate to misjudge her footing, and she lurched sideways, stumbling into the living room.

When she stood upright, Ox sat up on the sofa. "Are you okay?"

River appeared and dropped his ball at Kate's feet.

"I guess I'm good enough to play fetch." She laughed.

Matt kissed Ali on the lips, and she rested her head against his chest. "If you wouldn't mind printing me out a new boarding pass. I'm going to need it."

And Kate swore she'd never seen her best friend smile like *that* before.

Epilogue

TWO YEARS LATER

"Have you seen my hair clip?" Kate asked Ox over the sound of the kitchen's stand mixer.

"I think I saw it on your nightstand." At the table, Ox scraped the bowl down around the edges.

"I looked there and couldn't find it." Kate placed her hands on her hips.

On a high humidity day, like today, her copper curls nearly engulfed her face if she didn't put them up.

"What time are Ali and Matt arriving?" Ox studied the recipe for the next step. It was his first time making a three-tier wedding cake.

"Their flight from Australia to Seattle comes in around four, and then they should be landing at the Crooked River Airport about six. I think there's an hour gap between the two." Kate poured them both some pomegranate iced tea and handed a glass to Ox.

Bayou snored loudly from his bed in the kitchen. He slept a lot more these days, but he'd earned it. His work with the chemotherapy department at the hospital kept him busy. They even had his picture next to his service award in the waiting room.

River laid near Bayou's bed, his chin pressed flat against the hardwood floor, trying to cool off after another round of fetch. His green ball rested between his paw and his whiskers.

Ox and Kate had a drawer full of backups just in case one got lost. They'd made that mistake once, and it was enough to teach them that River only loved one ball — the green one — and imitations would not be accepted.

"Ali's wedding dress should be delivered this afternoon from France or someplace in that area. Can you believe they're getting married?"

"I can believe it." Ox took a chug of tea and measured the baking soda and baking powder, careful not to confuse the two. "What I can't believe is they want to get married here, at the inn, and trusted me to make their cake."

"Homemade cake doesn't go with an elegant wedding dress from France, does it?" Kate leaned down and kissed Ox softly on the lips.

"Your kisses are sweeter than this cake."

Kate blushed and heard a whimpering sound coming from the master bedroom. "I guess they're up."

She set her glass on the table and hurried down the hall.

When Kate returned, she had the rescued mutt puppies in each of her arms' crook. Their black, tan, and white fur made them appear to be a mix of Bernese Mountain Dog and Labrador.

"You can't keep babying them like that, Kate," Ox warned, taking the breaks off his wheelchair and wheeled toward Kate. "They're dogs, not infants."

She kissed the tops of both the puppies' heads. "But they're our babies."

Ox reached his arms out, and she set the puppies on the floor. Kate wrapped her arms around her husband's neck and lowered herself into his lap. She pressed her cheek against his and closed her eyes for a moment.

"Oh, I think they need to go potty," Ox mumbled.

Kate climbed off his lap and held open the front door. Ox wheeled over and lined up with the ramp.

"Come on, Zeus and Apollo, let's go potty." Ox waved the puppies forward, and they stumbled down the ramp, followed by his wheelchair.

Once at the ramp's bottom, he turned and looked back at Kate standing in the doorway. River appeared at her side, followed by Bayou on her other.

"I love you!" Ox called with a smile.

She blew him a kiss. "I love you, too."

"I meant River and Bayou, but yes, you also, Kate."

She screeched with delight and bolted down the ramp as Ox tried his best to wheel away. Laughter filled the front yard just as she caught Ox and kissed him.

The End

Did you love this story? Maybe it wasn't right for you? Either way, I loved love to hear from you!! A quick minute to write a review would mean a great deal to me and help future readers discover this book. Please and thank you!

Kate's Less-Dairy Chicken Lasagna

Serves 2

- 3 oven-ready lasagna noodles (about 12 in a small box) (no-bake)

- 1 can of tomato sauce (15 oz)

- 1 cup fresh spinach

- ½ cup shredded mozzarella + ¼ cup

- 1 cup cooked and diced up chicken

- 4 cloves fresh garlic (minced)

- ½ teaspoon oregano (dried)

- ½ teaspoon onion (dried)

- 1 tablespoon parsley (dried)

- Salt and pepper to taste

- Butter bottom of a 7x5x1.5 oven-safe glass dish

- Mix tomato sauce, spinach, chicken, garlic, oregano, parsley, salt, pepper, and ½ cup mozzarella in a bowl.

- Place one of the noodles into the pan and spread ¼ of the mix on top. Follow with another noodle, another ¼ of the mix, and then another noodle, and ¼ of the mix, then top with the ¼ cup mozzarella.

- Cover with foil and place in preheated oven at 350°F for 20 minutes, then remove the foil and cook for about 5-10 minutes until cheese on top melts and starts to brown.

- Remove and let stand for 5 minutes before serving.

Kate's Emergency Girls' Party Playlist

Find the playlist on YouTube by clicking here.

Maren Morris - *I COULD USE A LOVE SONG*

Pistol Annies - *HELL ON HEELS*

Shania Twain - *WHOSE BED HAVE YOUR BOOTS BEEN UNDER*

Neil Sedaka - *CALENDAR GIRL*

Tammy Wynette - *'TIL I CAN MAKE IT ON MY OWN*

Reba McEntire - *THE HEART IS A LONELY HUNTER*

Keith Urban - *DAYS GO BY*

Miranda Lambert with Carrie Underwood - *SOMETHIN' BAD*

Lori McKenna - *BIBLE SONG*

Kenny Chesney - *NO SHOES, NO SHIRT, NO PROBLEM*

Miranda Lambert - *VICE*

Chris Stapleton - *STARTING OVER*

Carrie Underwood - *DRINKING ALONE*

Gary Allan - *EVERY STORM RUNS OUT OF RAIN*

Acknowledgments

A big long-distance hug and thank you to my ***Happy PAWS Readers*** ~ Caroline at Page-Turners, Carol Harris, JoDena Pysher, and Carrie Thompson.

A big SHOUT OUT to Linda Martin, April Greer, Bambi Rathman, Sam Alvarez, Joyce Stewart, Durene Adams, Starla DeKruyf, Lisa Small, Tina Meyers, Rachael Bloome (and Mariposa Coffee), Dyana Hulgan, and Betty Taylor for your continued support for my books.

A special thank you to Carla Vergot & Carla Vergot's Back Porch, Annette G. Anders, Jamie Rutland Gillespie, Laura LaTulipe, and Denise Birt. Your drive to spread kind words about my books, along with your mirrored frustration for my stolen novel, was heartwarming.

For Ransom, a basket of balls since he only had 87,439 rounds of fetch instead of 89,439 because I was on a deadline for this novel.

And to D.S. ~ Thank you for your unwavering support, guidance, knowledge, and love, which allows me to showcase the best of myself.

About the Author

 Savannah Hendricks (born in California, raised in Washington, and resides in Arizona) is a full-time social worker and fills as much of her weekends as possible with writing. She loves all things dog-related and has a passion for red wine. Savannah enjoys gardening, baking, and creating yummy recipes. You'll often find her hollering at the TV during restoration shows when they paint over red bricks.

If you'd love a digital personalized autograph or bookplate, you can request one by visiting: savannahhendricks.com
Please discover more about Savannah by interacting with her on:

Instagram: savannahhendricks_author
Facebook: AuthorSavannahHendricks

Also By Savannah

<u>Heartfelt Coming of Age/Women's Fiction</u>
Sun City, 85373
The Album (Multi-Award-Winning)
I Adopted My Mom at the Bus Station (Multi-Award-Winning)

<u>Humorously Wholesome Romance</u>
Route to Romance
A Hearts of Woolsey series: A Desert Restoration, A Desert Romance, A Desert Rivalry
The Christmas Rental
Grounded in January (Award-Winning)
Grounded in July
To Work Out or to Wed

Meaningful Picture Books

Where Does "I Love You" Go?

The Needle-less Christmas Tree & Other Tree Tales

Winston Versus the Snow (Multi-Award-Winning)

Nonnie and I (Available in English, Spanish & Bilingual)